The ge

as the dirt piled higher and higher around them, in a circular mound like a crater. Summer neared its end, and on one stormy day dirt and rubble rose above the parapets and began to spill over into the courts and piazzas: Janeil must soon be buried and all within suffocated. It was then that a group of impulsive cadets, with more élan than dignity, took up weapons and charged up the slope. The Meks dumped dirt and stone upon them, but a handful gained the ridge where they fought in a kind of dreadful exaltation.

Fifteen minutes the fight raged and the earth became sodden with rain and blood. For one glorious moment the cadets swept the ridge clear, and had not most of their fellows been lost under the rubble, anything might have occurred. But the Meks regrouped and thrust forward. Ten men were left, then six, then four, then one, then none. The Meks marched down the slope, swarmed over the battlements, and with somber intensity killed all within. Janeil, for seven hundred years the abode of gallant gentlemen and gracious ladies, had become a lifeless hulk.

The Tor SF Doubles

A Meeting with Medusa/Green Mars, Arthur C. Clarke/Kim Stanley Robinson • **Hardfought/Cascade Point**, Greg Bear/Timothy Zahn • **Born with the Dead/The Saliva Tree**, Robert Silverberg/Brian W. Aldiss • **Tango Charlie and Foxtrot Romeo/The Star Pit**, John Varley/Samuel R. Delany • **No Truce with Kings/Ship of Shadows**, Poul Anderson/Fritz Leiber • **Enemy Mine/Another Orphan**, Barry B. Longyear/John Kessel • **Screwtop/The Girl Who Was Plugged In**, Vonda N. McIntyre/James Tiptree, Jr. • **The Nemesis from Terra/Battle for the Stars**, Leigh Brackett/Edmond Hamilton • **The Ugly Little Boy/The [Widget], the [Wadget], and Boff**, Isaac Asimov/Theodore Sturgeon • **Sailing to Byzantium/Seven American Nights**, Robert Silverberg/Gene Wolfe • **Houston, Houston, Do You Read?/Souls**, James Tiptree, Jr./Joanna Russ • **He Who Shapes/The Infinity Box**, Roger Zelazny/Kate Wilhelm • **The Blind Geometer/The New Atlantis**, Kim Stanley Robinson/Ursula K. Le Guin • **The Saturn Game/Iceborn**, Poul Anderson/Gregory Benford & Paul A. Carter • **The Last Castle/Nightwings**, Jack Vance/Robert Silverberg • **The Color of Neanderthal Eyes/And Strange at Ecbatan the Trees**, James Tiptree, Jr./Michael Bishop* • **Divide and Rule/The Sword of Rhiannon**, L. Sprague de Camp/Leigh Brackett* • **In Another Country/Vintage Season**, Robert Silverberg/C. L. Moore* • **Ill Met in Lankhmar/The Fair at Emain Macha**, Fritz Leiber/Charles de Lint* • **The Pugnacious Peacemaker/The Wheels of If**, Harry Turtledove/L. Sprague de Camp*

**forthcoming*

JACK VANCE

THE LAST CASTLE

A TOM DOHERTY ASSOCIATES BOOK
NEW YORK

This book is a work of fiction. All the characters and events portrayed in it are fictional, and any resemblance to real people or incidents is purely coincidental.

THE LAST CASTLE

A Tor Book
Published by Tom Doherty Associates, Inc.
49 West 24th Street
New York, N.Y. 10010

Cover art by Brian Waugh

ISBN: 0-812-50194-2 Can. ISBN: 0-812-50274-4

First Tor edition: December 1989

Printed in the United States of America

0 9 8 7 6 5 4 3 2 1

I

1.

Toward the end of a stormy summer afternoon, with the sun finally breaking out under ragged black rain-clouds, Castle Janeil was overwhelmed and its population destroyed. Until almost the last moment factions among the castle clans contended as to how Destiny properly should be met. The gentlemen of most prestige and account elected to ignore the entire undignified circumstance and went about their normal pursuits, with neither more nor less punctilio than usual. A few cadets, desperate to the point of hysteria, took up weapons and prepared to resist the final assault. Still others, perhaps a quarter of the total population, waited passively, ready—almost happy—to expiate the sins of the human race. In the end, death came uniformly to all, and all extracted as much satisfaction from their dying as this essentially graceless process could afford. The proud sat turning the pages of their beautiful books, discussing the qualities of a century-old essence, or fondling a favorite Phane, and died without deigning to heed the fact. The hotheads raced up the muddy slope which, outraging all normal rationality, loomed above the parapets of Janeil. Most were buried under sliding rubble, but a few gained the ridge to gun, hack and stab, until they themselves were shot, crushed by the half-alive power-wagons, hacked or stabbed. The contrite waited in the classic posture of expiation—on their knees, heads bowed—and perished, so they believed, by a process in which the Meks were symbols and human sin the reality. In the end all were dead: gentlemen, ladies, Phanes in the pavilions; Peasants in the stables. Of all those who had inhabited Janeil, only the Birds survived, creatures awkward, gauche and raucous, oblivious to pride and faith, more concerned with the wholeness of their hides than the dignity of their castle. As the Meks swarmed down over the parapets, the Birds departed their cotes and, screaming strident insults, flapped east toward Hagedorn, now the last castle of Earth.

2.

Four months before, the Meks had appeared in the park before Janeil, fresh from the Sea Island massacre. Climbing to the turrets and balconies, sauntering the Sunset Promenade, from ramparts and parapets, the gentlemen and ladies of Janeil, some two thousand in all, looked down at the brown-gold warriors. Their mood was complex—amused indifference, flippant disdain, and a substratum of doubt and foreboding; all the product of three basic circumstances—their own exquisitely subtle civilization, the security provided by Janeil's walls, and the fact that they could conceive no recourse, no means for altering circumstances.

The Janeil Meks had long since departed to join the revolt; there remained only Phanes, Peasants and Birds from which to fashion what would have been the travesty of a punitive force. Janeil was deemed impregnable. The walls, two hundred feet tall, were black rock-melt contained in the meshes of a silver-blue steel alloy. Solar cells provided energy for all the needs of the castle, and in the event of emergency, food could be synthesized from carbon dioxide and water vapor, as well as syrup for Phanes, Peasants and Birds. Such a need was not envisaged. Janeil was self-sufficient and secure, though inconveniences might arise when machinery broke down and there were no Meks to repair it. The situation then was disturbing but hardly desperate. During the day the gentlemen so inclined brought forth energy-guns and sport-rifles and killed as many Meks as the extreme range allowed.

After dark the Meks brought forward power-wagons and earth-movers, and began to raise a dike around Janeil. The folk of the castle watched without comprehension until the dike reached a height of fifty feet and dirt began to spill down against the walls. Then the dire purpose of the Meks became apparent, and insouciance gave way to dismal foreboding. All the gentlemen of Janeil were erudite in at least one realm of knowledge; certain were mathematical theoreticians, while others had made a profound study of the physical sciences. Some of these, with a detail of Peasants to perform the sheerly physical exertion, attempted to restore the energy-cannon to functioning condition. Unluckily, the cannon had not been maintained in good order. Various components were obviously corroded or damaged. Conceivably these components might have been replaced from the Mek shops on the second sublevel, but none of the group had any knowledge of the Mek nomenclature or warehousing system. Warrick Madency Arban (Arban of the Madency family in the Warrick clan) suggested that a work-force of Peasants search the warehouse, but in view of the limited mental capacity of the Peasants, nothing was done and the whole plan to restore the energy-cannon came to naught.

The gentlefolk of Janeil watched in fascination as the dirt piled higher and higher around them, in a circular mound like a crater. Summer neared its end, and on one stormy day dirt and rubble rose above the parapets, and began to spill over into the courts and piazzas: Janeil must soon be buried and all within suffocated. It was then that a group of impulsive young cadets, with more élan than dignity, took up weapons and charged up the slope. The Meks dumped dirt and stone upon them, but a handful gained the ridge where they fought in a kind of dreadful exaltation.

Fifteen minutes the fight raged and the earth became sodden with rain and blood. For one glorious moment the cadets swept the ridge clear, and had not most of their fellows been lost under the rubble, anything might have occurred. But the Meks regrouped and thrust forward. Ten men were left, then six, then four, then one, then none. The Meks marched down the slope, swarmed over the battlements, and with somber intensity killed all within. Janeil, for seven hundred years the abode of gallant gentlemen, and gracious ladies, had become a lifeless hulk.

3.

The Mek, standing as if a specimen in a museum case, was a manlike creature, native, in his original version, to a planet of Etamin. His tough rusty-bronze hide glistened metallically as if oiled or waxed; the spines thrusting back from scalp and neck shone like gold, and indeed were coated with a conductive copper-chrome film. His sense organs were gathered in clusters at the site of a man's ears; his visage—it was often a shock, walking the lower corridors, to come suddenly upon a Mek—was corrugated muscle, not dissimilar to the look of an uncovered human brain. His maw, a vertical irregular cleft at the base of this "face," was an obsolete organ by reason of the syrup sac which had been introduced under the skin of the shoulders; the digestive organs, originally used to extract nutrition from decayed swamp vegetation and coelenterates, had atrophied. The Mek typically wore no garment except possibly a work-apron or a tool-belt, and in the sunlight his rust-bronze skin made a handsome display. This was the Mek solitary, a creature intrinsically as effective as man—perhaps more by virtue of his superb brain which also functioned as a radio transceiver. Working in the mass, by the teeming thousands, he seemed less admirable, less competent: a hybrid of subman and cockroach.

Certain savants, notably Morninglight's D.R. Jardine and Salonson of Tuang, considered the Mek bland and phlegmatic, but the profound Claghorn of Castle Hagedorn asserted otherwise. The emotions of the Mek, said Claghorn, were different from human emotions, and only vaguely comprehensible to man. After diligent research Claghorn isolated over a dozen Mek emotions.

In spite of such research, the Mek revolt

came as an utter surprise, no less to Claghorn, D.R. Jardine and Salonson than to anyone else. Why? asked everyone. How could a group so long submissive have contrived so murderous a plot?

The most reasonable conjecture was also the simplest: the Mek resented servitude and hated the Earthmen who had removed him from his natural environment. Those who argued against this theory claimed that it projected human emotions and attitudes into a nonhuman organism, that the Mek had every reason to feel gratitude toward the gentlemen who had liberated him from the conditions of Etamin Nine. To this, the first group would inquire, "Who projects human attitudes now?" And the retort of their opponents was often, "Since no one knows for certain, one projection is no more absurd than another."

II

1.

Castle Hagedorn occupied the crest of a black diorite crag overlooking a wide valley to the south. Larger, more majestic than Janeil, Hagedorn was protected by walls a mile in circumference, and three hundred feet tall. The parapets stood a full nine hundred feet above the valley, with towers, turrets and observation aeries rising even higher. Two sides of the crag, at east and west, dropped sheer to the valley. The north and south slopes, a trifle less steep, were terraced and planted with vines, artichokes, pears and pomegranates. An avenue rising from the valley circled the crag and passed through a portal into the central plaza. Opposite stood the great Rotunda, with at either side the tall Houses of the twenty-eight families.

The original castle, constructed immediately after the return of men to Earth, stood on the site now occupied by the plaza. The tenth Hagedorn, assembling an enormous force of Peasants and Meks, had built the new walls, after which he demolished the old castle. The twenty-eight Houses dated from this time, five hundred years before.

The clans of Hagedorn, their colors and associated families:

CLANS	COLORS	FAMILIES
Xanten	yellow; black piping	Haude, Quay, Idelsea, Esledune, Salonson, Roseth.
Beaudry	dark blue; white piping	Onwane, Zadig, Prine, Fer, Sesune.
Overwhele	gray, green; red rosettes	Claghorn, Abreu, Woss, Hinken, Zumbeld
Aure	brown, black	Zadhause, Fotergil, Marune, Baudune, Godalming, Lesmanic.
Isseth	purple, dark red	Mazeth, Floy, Luder-Hepman, Uegus, Kerrithew, Bethune.

The first gentleman of the castle, elected for life, is known as "Hagedorn."

The clan chief, selected by the family elders, bears the name of his clan, thus: "Xanten," "Beaudry," "Overwhele," "Aure," Isseth"—both clans and clan chiefs.

The family elder, selected by household heads, bears the name of his family. Thus "Idelsea," "Zadhause," "Bethune," and "Claghorn," are both families and family elders.

The remaining gentlemen and ladies bear first the clan, then the family, then the personal name. Thus: Aure Zadhause Ludwick, abbreviated to A.Z. Ludwick, and Beaudry Fer Dariane, abbreviated to B.F. Dariane.

Below the plaza were three service levels: the stables and garages at the bottom, next the Mek shops and Mek living quarters, then the various storerooms, warehouses and special shops—bakery, brewery, lapidary, arsenal, repository and the like.

The current Hagedorn, twenty-sixth of the line, was a Claghorn of the Overwheles. His selection had occasioned general surprise, because O.C. Charle, as he had been before his elevation, was a gentleman of no remarkable presence. His elegance, flair and erudition were only ordinary; he had never been notable for any significant originality of thought. His physical proportions were good; his face was square and bony, with a short straight nose, a benign brow and narrow gray eyes. His expression, normally a trifle abstracted—his detractors used the word "vacant"—by a simple lowering of the eyelids, a downward twitch of the coarse blond eyebrows at once became stubborn and surly, a fact of which O.C. Charle, or Hagedorn, was unaware.

The office, while exerting little or no formal authority, exerted a pervasive influence, and the style of the gentleman who was Hagedorn affected everyone. For this reason the selection of Hagedorn was a matter of no small importance, subject to hundreds of considerations, and it was the rare candidate who failed to have some old solecism or gaucherie discussed with embarrassing candor. While the candidate might never take overt umbrage, friendships were inevitably sundered, rancors augmented, reputations blasted. O.C. Charle's elevation represented a compromise between two factions among the Overwheles, to which clan the privilege of selection had fallen.

The gentlemen between whom O.C. Charle represented a compromise were both highly respected, but distinguished by basically different attitudes toward existence. The first was the talented Garr of the Zumbeld family. He exemplified the traditional virtues of Castle Hagedorn: he was a notable connoisseur of essences, and he dressed with absolute savoir, with never so much as a pleat nor a twist of the characteristic Overwhele rosette awry. He combined insouciance and flair with dignity; his repartee coruscated with brilliant allusions and turns of phrase; whcn aroused his wit was utterly mordant. He could quote every literary work of consequence; he performed expertly upon the nine-stringed lute, and was thus in constant demand at the Viewing of Antique Tabards. He was an antiquarian of unchallenged erudition and knew the locale of every major city of Old Earth, and could discourse for hours upon the history of the ancient times. His military expertise was unparalleled at Hagedorn, and challenged only by D.K. Magdah of Castle Delora and perhaps Brusham of Tuang. Faults? Flaws? Few could be cited: over-punctilio which might be construed as waspishness; an intrepid pertinacity which could be considered ruthlessness. O.Z. Garr could never be dismissed as insipid or indecisive, and his personal courage was beyond dispute. Two years before, a stray band of Nomads had ventured into Lucerne Valley, slaughtering Peasants, stealing cattle and going so far as to fire an arrow into the chest of an Isseth cadet. O.Z. Garr instantly assembled a punitive company of Meks, loaded them aboard a dozen power-wagons, and set forth in pursuit of the Nomads, finally overtaking them near Drene River, by the ruins of Worster Cathedral. The Nomads were unexpectedly strong, unexpectedly crafty, and were not content to turn tail and flee. During the fighting, O.Z. Garr displayed the most exemplary demeanor, directing the attack from the seat of his power-wagon, a pair of Meks standing by with shields to ward away arrows. The conflict ended in a rout of the Nomads; they left twenty-seven lean, black-cloaked corpses strewn on the field, while only twenty Meks lost their lives.

O.Z. Garr's opponent in the election was Claghorn, elder of the Claghorn family. As with O.Z. Garr, the exquisite discriminations of Hagedorn society came to Claghorn as easily as swimming to a fish. He was no less erudite than O.Z. Garr, though hardly so versatile, his principle field of study being the Meks, their physiology, linguistic modes, and social patterns. Claghorn's conversation was more profound, but less entertaining and not so trenchant as that of O.Z. Garr; he seldom employed the extravagant tropes and allusions which characterized Garr's discussions, preferring a style of speech which was unadorned. Claghorn kept no Phanes; O.Z. Garr's four matched Gossamer Dainties were marvels of delight, and at the Viewing of Antique Tabards Garr's presentations were seldom outshone. The important contrast between the two men lay in their philosophic outlook. O.Z. Garr, a traditionalist, a fervent exemplar of his society, subscribed to its tenets without reservation. He was beset by neither doubt nor guilt; he felt no desire to alter the conditions which afforded more than two thousand gentlemen and ladies lives of great richness. Claghorn, while by no means an Expiationist, was known to feel dissatisfaction with the general tenor of life at Castle Hagedorn, and argued so plausibly that many folk refused to listen to him, on the grounds that they became uncomfortable. But an indefinable malaise ran deep, and Claghorn had many influential supporters.

When the time came for ballots to be cast, neither O.Z. Garr nor Claghorn could muster sufficient support. The office finally was conferred upon a gentleman who never in his most optimistic reckonings had expected it—a gentleman of decorum and dignity but no great depth; without flippancy, but likewise without vivacity; affable but disinclined to force an issue to a disagreeable conclusion: O.C. Charle, the new Hagedorn.

Six months later, during the dark hours before dawn, the Hagedorn Meks evacuated their quarters and departed, taking with them power-wagons, tools, weapons and electrical equipment. The act had clearly been long in the planning, for simultaneously the Meks at each of the eight other castles made a similar departure.

The initial reaction at Castle Hagedorn, as elsewhere, was incredulity, then shocked anger, then—when the implications of the act were pondered—a sense of foreboding and calamity.

The new Hagedorn, the clan chiefs and certain other notables appointed by Hagedorn met in the formal council chamber to consider the matter. They sat around a great table covered with red velvet: Hagedorn at the head; Xanten and Isseth at his left; Overwhele, Aure and Beaudry at his right; then the others, including O.Z. Garr, I.K. Linus, A.G. Bernal, a mathematical theoretician of great ability, and B.F. Wyas, an equally sagacious antiquarian who had identified the sites of many ancient cities—Palmyra, Lübeck, Eridu, Zanesville, Burton-on-Trent and Massilia, among others. Certain family elders filled out the council: Marune and Baudune of Aure; Quay, Roseth and Idelsea of Xanten; Uegus of Isseth, Claghorn of Overwhele.

All sat silent for a period of ten minutes, arranging their minds and performing the silent act of psychic accommodations known as "intression."

At last Hagedorn spoke. "The castle is suddenly bereft of its Meks. Needless to say, this is an inconvenient condition, to be adjusted as swiftly as possible. Here, I am sure, we find ourselves of one mind."

He looked around the table. All thrust forward carved ivory tablets to signify assent—all save Claghorn, who however did not stand it on end to signify dissent.

Isseth, a stern white-haired gentleman magnificently handsome in spite of his seventy years, spoke in a grim voice. "I see no point in cogitation or delay. What we must do is clear. Admittedly the Peasants are poor material from which to recruit an armed force. Nonetheless, we must assemble them, equip them with sandals, smocks and weapons so that they do not discredit us, and put them under good leadership: O.Z. Garr or Xanten. Birds can locate the vagrants, whereupon we will track them down, order the Peasants to give them a good drubbing, and herd them home on the double."

Xanten, thirty-five years old—extraordinarily young to be a clan chief—and a notorious firebrand, shook his head. "The idea is appealing but impractical. Peasants simply could not stand up to the Meks, no matter how we trained them."

The statement was manifestly accurate. The Peasants, small andromorphs originally of Spica Ten, were not so much timid as incapable of performing a vicious act.

A dour silence held the table. O.Z. Garr finally spoke. "The dogs have stolen our powerwagons, otherwise I'd be tempted to ride out and chivy the rascals home with a whip."[1]

1. This, only an approximate translation, fails to capture the pungency of the language. Several words have no con-

"A matter of perplexity," said Hagedorn, "is syrup. Naturally they carried away what they could. When this is exhausted—what then? Will they starve? Impossible for them to return to their original diet. What was it? Swamp mud? Eh, Claghorn, you're the expert in these matters. Can the Meks return to a diet of mud?"

"No," said Claghorn. "The organs of the adult are atrophied. If a cub were started on the diet, he'd probably survive."

"Just as I assumed." Hagedorn scowled portentously down at his clasped hands to conceal his total lack of any constructive proposal.

A gentleman in the dark blue of the Beaudrys appeared in the doorway; he poised himself, held high his right arm and bowed so that the fingers swept the floor.

Hagedorn rose to his feet. "Come forward, B.F. Robarth; what is your news?" For this

temporary equivalents. "Skirkling" as in "to send skirkling," denotes a frantic pell-mell flight in all directions, accompanied by a vibration or twinkling or jerking motion. To "volith" is to toy idly with a matter, the implication being that the person involved is of such Jovian potency that all difficulties dwindle to contemptible triviality. "Raudlebogs" are the semi-intelligent beings of Etamin Four, who were brought to Earth, trained first as gardeners, then construction workers, then sent home in disgrace because of certain repulsive habits they refused to forego.

The statement of O.Z. Garr, therefore, becomes something like this: "Were power-wagons at hand, I'd volith riding forth with a whip to send the raudlebogs skirkling home."

was the significance of the newcomer's genuflection.

"The news is a message broadcast from Halcyon. The Meks have attacked; they have fired the structure and are slaughtering all. The radio went dead one minute ago."

All swung around, some jumped to their feet. "Slaughter?" croaked Claghorn.

"I am certain that by now Halcyon is no more."

Claghorn sat staring with eyes unfocused. The others discussed the dire news in voices heavy with horror.

Hagedorn once more brought the council back to order. "This is clearly an extreme situation—the gravest, perhaps, of our entire history. I am frank to state that I can suggest no decisive counter-act."

Overwhele inquired, "What of the other castles? Are they secure?"

Hagedorn turned to B.F. Robarth. "Will you be good enough to make general radio contact with all other castles, and inquire as to their condition?"

Xanten said, "Others are as vulnerable as Halcyon: Sea Island and Delora, in particular, and Maraval as well."

Claghorn emerged from his reverie. "The gentlemen and ladies of these places, in my opinion, should consider taking refuge at Janeil or here, until the uprising is quelled."

Others around the table looked at him in surprise and puzzlement. O.Z. Garr inquired in the silkiest of voices: "You envision the gentlefolk of these castles scampering to refuge at the cock-a-hoop swaggering of the lower orders?"

"Indeed, should they wish to survive," responded Claghorn politely. A gentleman of late middle age, Claghorn was stocky and strong, with black-gray hair, magnificent green eyes, and a manner which suggested great internal force under stern control. "Flight by definition entails a certain diminution of dignity," he went on to say. "If O.Z. Garr can propound an elegant manner of taking to one's heels, I will be glad to learn it, and everyone else should likewise heed, because in the days to come the capability may be of comfort to all."

Hagedorn interposed before O.Z. Garr could reply. "Let us keep to the issues. I confess I cannot see to the end of all this. The Meks have demonstrated themselves to be murderers; how can we take them back into our service? But if we don't—well, to say the least, conditions will be austere until we can locate and train a new force of technicians. We must consider along these lines."

"The spaceships!" exclaimed Xanten. "We must see to them at once!"

"What's this?" inquired Beaudry, a gentleman of rock-hard face. "How do you mean, 'see to them'?"

"They must be protected from damage! What else? They are our link to the Home Worlds. The maintenance Meks probably have not deserted the hangars, since if they propose to exterminate us, they will want to deny us the spaceships."

"Perhaps you care to march with a levy of Peasants to take the hangars under firm control?" suggested O.Z. Garr in a somewhat supercilious voice. A long history of rivalry and mutual detestation existed between himself and Xanten.

"It may be our only hope," said Xanten. "Still—how does one fight with a levy of Peasants? Better that I fly to the hangars and reconnoiter. Meanwhile, perhaps you, and others with military expertise, will take in hand the recruitment and training of a Peasant militia."

"In this regard," stated O.Z. Garr, "I await the outcome of our current deliberations. If it develops that there lies the optimum course, I naturally will apply my competences to the fullest degree. If your own capabilities are best fulfilled by spying out the activities of the Meks, I hope that you will be largehearted enough to do the same."

The two gentlemen glared at each other. A year previously their enmity had almost culminated in a duel. Xanten, a gentleman tall, clean-limbed and nervously active, was gifted with great natural flair, but likewise evinced a disposition too easy for absolute elegance. The traditionalists considered him "sthross," indicating a manner flawed by an almost imperceptible slackness and lack of punctilio: not the best possible choice for clan chief.

Xanten's response to O.Z. Garr was blandly polite. "I shall be glad to take this task upon myself. Since haste is of the essence I will risk the accusation of precipitousness and leave at once. Hopefully I return to report tomorrow." He rose, performed a ceremonious bow to Hagedorn, another all-inclusive salute to the council and departed.

He crossed to Esledune House, where he maintained an apartment on the thirteenth level: four rooms furnished in the style known as Fifth Dynasty, after an epoch in the history of the Altair Home Planets, from which the human race had returned to Earth. His current consort, Araminta, a lady of the Onwane family, was absent on affairs of her own, which suited Xanten well enough. After plying him with questions she would have discredited his simple explanation, preferring to suspect an assignation at his country place. Truth to tell, he had become bored with Araminta and had reason to believe that she felt similarly—or perhaps his exalted rank had provided her less opportunity to preside at glittering social functions than she had expected. They had bred no children. Araminta's daughter by a previous connection had been tallied to her. Her second child must then be tallied to Xanten, preventing him from siring another child.[2]

Xanten doffed his yellow council vestments, and, assisted by a young Peasant buck,

2. The population of Castle Hagedorn was fixed; each gentleman and each lady was permitted a single child. If by chance another were born the parent must either find someone who had not yet sired to sponsor it, or dispose of it another way. The usual procedure was to give the child into the care of the Expiationists.

donned dark yellow hunting-breeches with black trim, a black jacket, black boots. He drew a cap of soft black leather over his head, and slung a pouch over his shoulder, into which he loaded weapons: a coiled blade, an energy-gun.

Leaving the apartment, he summoned the lift and descended to the first-level armory, where normally a Mek clerk would have served him. Now Xanten, to his vast disgust, was forced to take himself behind the counter, and rummage here and there. The Meks had removed most of the sport-rifles, all the pellet ejectors and heavy energy-guns; an ominous circumstance, thought Xanten. At last he found a steel slingwhip, spare power slugs for his gun, a brace of fire grenades and a high-powered monocular.

He returned to the lift and rode to the top level, ruefully considering the long climb when eventually the mechanism broke down, with no Meks at hand to make repairs. He thought of the apoplectic furies of rigid traditionalists such as Beaudry and chuckled: eventful days lay ahead!

Stopping at the top level, he crossed to the parapets and proceeded around to the radio room. Customarily three Mek specialists connected into the apparatus by wires clipped to their quills sat typing messages as they arrived; now B.F. Robarth stood before the mechanism, uncertainly twisting the dials, his mouth wry with deprecation and distaste for the job.

"Any further news?" Xanten asked.

B.F. Robarth gave him a sour grin. "The folk at the other end seem no more familiar with this cursed tangle than I. I hear occasional voices. I believe that the Meks are attacking Castle Delora."

Claghorn had entered the room behind Xanten. "Did I hear you correctly? Delora Castle is gone?"

"Not gone yet, Claghorn. But as good as gone. The Delora walls are little better than a picturesque crumble."

"Sickening situation!" muttered Xanten. "How can sentient creatures perform such evil? After all these centuries, how little we actually know of them!" As he spoke he recognized the tactlessness of his remark; Claghorn had devoted much time to a study of the Meks.

"The act itself is not astounding," said Claghorn shortly. "It has occurred a thousand times in human history."

Mildly surprised that Claghorn should use human history in reference to a case involving the suborders, Xanten asked, "You were never aware of this vicious aspect to the Mek nature?"

"No. Never. Never indeed."

Claghorn seemed unduly sensitive, thought Xanten. Understandable, all in all. Claghorn's basic doctrine as set forth during the Hagedorn selection was by no means simple, and Xanten neither understood it nor completely endorsed what he conceived to be its goals; but it was plain that the revolt of the Meks had cut the ground out from under

Claghorn's feet. Probably to the somewhat bitter satisfaction of O.Z. Garr, who must feel vindicated in his traditionalist doctrines.

Claghorn said tersely, "The life we've been leading couldn't last forever. It's a wonder it lasted as long as it did."

"Perhaps so," said Xanten in a soothing voice. "Well, no matter. All things change. Who knows? The Peasants may be planning to poison our food. . . . I must go." He bowed to Claghorn, who returned him a crisp nod, and to B.F. Robarth, then departed the room.

He climbed the spiral staircase—almost a ladder—to the cotes, where the Birds lived in an invincible disorder, occupying themselves with gambling, quarrels and a version of chess, with rules incomprehensible to every gentleman who had tried to understand it.

Castle Hagedorn maintained a hundred Birds, tended by a gang of long-suffering Peasants, whom the Birds held in vast disesteem. The Birds were garish, garrulous creatures, pigmented red, yellow or blue, with long necks, jerking inquisitive heads and an inherent irreverence which no amount of discipline or tutelage could overcome. Spying Xanten, they emitted a chorus of rude jeers: "Somebody wants a ride! Heavy thing!" "Why don't the self-anointed two-footers grow wings for themselves?" "My friend, never trust a Bird! We'll sky you, then fling you down on your fundament!"

"Quiet!" called Xanten. "I need six fast silent Birds for an important mission. Are any capable of such a task?"

"Are any capable, he asks!" *"A ros ros ros!* When none of us have flown for a week!" "Silence? We'll give you silence, yellow and black!"

"Come then. You. You. You of the wise eye. You there. You with the cocked shoulder. You with the green pompon. To the basket."

The Birds designated, jeering, grumbling, reviling the Peasants, allowed their syrup sacs to be filled, then flapped to the wicker seat where Xanten waited. "To the space depot at Vincenne," he told them. "Fly high and silently. Enemies are abroad. We must learn what harm if any has been done to the spaceships."

"To the depot, then!" Each Bird seized a length of rope tied to an overhead framework; the chair was yanked up with a jerk calculated to rattle Xanten's teeth, and off they flew, laughing, cursing each other for not supporting more of the load, but eventually all accommodating themselves to the task and flying with a coordinated flapping of the thirty-six sets of wings. To Xanten's relief, their garrulity lessened; silently they flew south, at a speed of fifty or sixty miles per hour.

The afternoon was already waning. The ancient countryside, scene to so many comings and goings, so much triumph and so much disaster, was laced with long black shadows. Looking down, Xanten reflected that though the human stock was native to this soil, and though his immediate ancestors had maintained their holdings for seven hundred years, Earth still seemed an alien world. The reason of course was by no means mysterious or rooted in paradox. After the Six-Star War, Earth had lain fallow for three thousand years, unpopulated save for a handful of anguished wretches who somehow had survived the cataclysm and who had become semibarbaric Nomads. Then seven hundred years ago certain rich lords of Altair, motivated to some extent by political disaffection, but no less by caprice, had decided to return to Earth. Such was the origin of the nine great strongholds, the resident gentlefolk and the staffs of specialized andromorphs. . . . Xanten flew over an area where an antiquarian had directed excavations, revealing a plaza flagged with white stone, a broken obelisk, a tumbled statue. . . . The sight, by some trick of association, stimulated Xanten's mind to an astonishing vision, so simple and yet so grand that he looked around, in all directions, with new eyes. The vision was Earth repopulated with men, the land cultivated, Nomads driven back into the wilderness.

At the moment the image was farfetched. And Xanten, watching the soft contours of Old Earth slide below, pondered the Mek revolt which had altered his life with such startling abruptness.

Claghorn had long insisted that no human condition endured forever, with the corollary that the more complicated such a condition, the greater its susceptibility to change. In which case the seven-hundred-year continuity of Castle Hagedorn—as artificial, extravagant and intricate as life could be—became an astonishing circumstance in itself. Claghorn had pushed his thesis further. Since change was inevitable, he argued that the gentlefolk should soften the impact by anticipating and controlling the changes—a doctrine which had been attacked with great fervor. The traditionalists labeled all of Claghorn's ideas demonstrable fallacy, and cited the very stability of castle life as proof of its viability. Xanten had inclined first one way, then the other, emotionally involved with neither cause. If anything, the fact of O.Z. Garr's traditionalism had nudged him toward Claghorn's views, and now it seemed as if events had vindicated Claghorn. Change had come, with an impact of the maximum harshness and violence.

There were still questions to be answered, of course. Why had the Meks chosen this particular time to revolt? Conditions had not altered appreciably for five hundred years, and the Meks had never previously hinted dissatisfaction. In fact they had revealed nothing of their feelings, though no one had ever troubled to ask them—save Claghorn.

The Birds were veering east to avoid the Ballarat Mountains, to the west of which were the ruins of a great city, never satisfactorily identified. Below lay the Lucerne Valley, at one time a fertile farmland. If one looked with great concentration, the outline of the various holdings could sometimes be distinguished. Ahead, the spaceship hangars were visible, where Mek technicians maintained four spaceships, jointly the property of Hagehorn, Janeil, Tuang, Morninglight and Maraval, though, for a variety of reasons, the ships were never used.

The sun was setting. Orange light twinkled and flickered on the metal walls. Xanten called instructions up to the Birds: "Circle down. Alight behind that line of trees, but fly low so that none will see."

Down on stiff wings curved the Birds, six ungainly necks stretched toward the ground. Xanten was ready for the impact; the Birds never seemed able to alight easily when they carried a gentleman. When the cargo was something in which they felt a personal concern, dandelion fluff would never have been disturbed by the jar.

Xanten expertly kept his balance, instead of tumbling and rolling in the manner preferred by the Birds. "You all have syrup," he told them. "Rest; make no noise; do not quarrel. By tomorrow's sunset, if I am not here, return to Castle Hagedorn and say that Xanten was killed."

"Never fear!" cried the Birds. "We will wait forever!" "At any rate till tomorrow's sunset!" "If danger threatens, if you are pressed—*a ros ros ros*! Call for the Birds." "*A ros!* We are ferocious when aroused!"

"I wish it were true," said Xanten. "The Birds are arrant cowards; this is well-known. Still, I value the sentiment. Remember my instructions, and quiet above all! I do not wish to be set upon and stabbed because of your clamor."

The Birds made indignant sounds. "Injustice, injustice! We are quiet as the dew!"

"Good." Xanten hurriedly moved away lest they should bellow new advice or reassurances after him.

Passing through the forest, he came to an open meadow at the far edge of which, perhaps a hundred yards distant, was the rear of the first hangar. He stopped to consider. Several factors were involved. First: the maintenance Meks, with the metal structure shielding them from radio contact, might still be unaware of the revolt. Hardly likely, he decided, in view of the otherwise careful planning. Second: the Meks, in continuous communication with their fellows, acted as a collective organism. The aggregate functions more competently than its parts, and the individual was not prone to initiative. Hence, vigilance was likely to be extreme. Third: if they expected anyone to attempt a discreet approach, they would necessarily scrutinize most closely the route which he proposed to take.

Xanten decided to wait in the shadows another ten minutes, until the setting sun shining over his shoulder should most effectively blind any who might watch.

Ten minutes passed. The hangars, burnished by the dying sunlight, bulked long, tall, completely quiet. In the intervening meadow long golden grass waved and rippled in a cool breeze. . . . Xanten took a deep breath, hefted his pouch, arranged his weapons and strode forth. It did not occur to him to crawl through the grass.

He reached the back of the nearest hangar without challenge. Pressing his ear to the metal he heard nothing. He walked to the corner, looked down the side: no sign of life. Xanten shrugged. Very well, then—to the door.

He walked beside the hangar, the setting sun casting a long black shadow ahead of him. He came to a door opening into the hangar administrative office. Since there was nothing to be gained by trepidation, Xanten thrust the door aside and entered.

The offices were empty. The desks, where centuries before underlings had sat, calculating invoices and bills of lading, were bare, polished free of dust. The computers and information banks, black enamel, glass, white and red switches, looked as if they had been installed only the day before.

Xanten crossed to a glass pane overlooking the hangar floor, shadowed under the bulk of the ship.

He saw no Meks. But on the floor of the hangar, arranged in neat rows and heaps, were elements and assemblies of the ship's control mechanism. Service panels gaped wide into the hull to show where the devices had been detached.

Xanten stepped from the office out into the hangar. The spaceship had been disabled, put out of commission. Xanten looked along the neat rows of parts. Certain savants of various castles were expert in the theory of space-time transfer; S.X. Rosenbox of Maraval had even derived a set of equations which, if translated into machinery, eliminated the troublesome Hamus effect. But not one gentleman, even were he so oblivious to personal honor as to touch a hand to a tool, would know how to replace, connect and tune the mechanisms heaped upon the hangar floor.

The malicious work had been done—when? Impossible to say.

Xanten returned to the office, stepped back out into the twilight, and walked to the next hangar. Again no Meks; again the spaceship had been gutted of its control mechanism. Xanten proceeded to the third hangar, where conditions were the same.

At the fourth hangar he discerned the faint sounds of activity. Stepping into the office, looking through the glass wall into the hangar, he found Meks working with their usual economy of motion, in a near-silence which was uncanny.

Xanten, already uncomfortable from skulking through the forest, became enraged by the cool destruction of his property. He strode forth into the hangar. Slapping his thigh to attract attention, he called in a harsh voice, "Return the components to place! How dare you vermin act in such a manner!"

The Meks turned about their black countenances to study him through black-headed lens-clusters at each side of their heads.

"What!" bellowed Xanten. "You hesitate?" He brought forth his steel whip, usually more of a symbolic adjunct than a punitive instrument, and slashed it against the ground. "Obey! This ridiculous revolt is at its end!"

The Meks still hesitated, and events wavered in the balance. None made a sound, though messages were passing among them, appraising the circumstances, establishing a consensus. Xanten could allow them no such leisure. He marched forward, wielding the whip, striking at the only area where the Meks felt pain: the ropy face. "To your duties," he roared. "A fine maintenance crew are you! A destruction crew is more like it!"

The Meks made the soft blowing sound which might mean anything. They fell back, and now Xanten noted one standing at the head of the companionway leading into the ship: a Mek larger than any he had seen before, and one in some fashion different. This Mek was aiming a pellet gun at his head. With an unhurried flourish, Xanten whipped away a Mek who had leaped forward with a knife, and without deigning to aim, fired at and destroyed the Mek who stood on the companionway, even as the slug sang past his head.

The other Meks were nevertheless committed to an attack. All surged forward. Lounging disdainfully against the hull, Xanten shot them as they came, moving his head once to avoid a chunk of metal, again reaching to catch a throw-knife and hurl it into the face of him who had thrown it.

The Meks drew back, and Xanten guessed that they had agreed on a new tactic: either to withdraw for weapons, or perhaps to confine him within the hangar. In any event no more could be accomplished here. He made play with the whip and cleared an avenue to the office. With tools, metal bars and forgings striking the glass behind him, he sauntered through the office and out into the night.

The full moon was rising: a great yellow globe casting a smoky saffron glow, like an antique lamp. Mek eyes were not well adapted for night-seeing, and Xanten waited by the door. Presently Meks began to pour forth, and Xanten hacked at their necks as they came.

The Meks drew back inside the hangar. Wiping his blade, Xanten strode off the way he had come, looking neither right nor left. He stopped short. The night was young. Something tickled his mind: the recollection of the Mek who had fired the pellet gun. He had been larger, possibly a darker bronze, but, more significantly, he had displayed an indefinable poise, almost authority—though such a word, when used in connection with the Meks, was anomalous. On the other hand, someone must have planned the revolt, or at least originated the concept. It might be worthwhile to extend the reconnaissance, though his primary information had been secured.

Xanten turned back and crossed the landing area to the barracks and garages. Once more, frowning in discomfort, he felt the need for discretion. What times these were! when a gentleman must skulk to avoid such as the Meks! He stole up behind the garages where a half dozen power-wagons[3] lay dozing.

Xanten looked them over. All were of the same sort, a metal frame with four wheels, an earth-moving blade at the front. Nearby must be the syrup stock. Xanten presently found a bin containing a number of canisters. He loaded a dozen on a nearby wagon, slashed the rest with his knife, so that the syrup gushed across the ground. The Meks used a somewhat different formulation; their syrup would be stocked at a different locale, presumably inside the barracks.

Xanten mounted a power-wagon, twisted the *awake* key, tapped the *go* button and pulled a lever which set the wheels into reverse motion. The power-wagon lurched back. Xanten halted it, turned it so that it faced the barracks. He did likewise with three others, then set them all into motion, one after the other. They trundled forward; the blades cut open the metal wall of the barracks, the roof sagged. The power-wagons continued, pushing the length of the interior, crushing all in their way.

3. Power-wagons, like the Meks, originally swamp-creatures from Etamin Nine, were great rectangular slabs of muscle, slung into a rectangular frame and protected from sunlight, insects and rodents by a synthetic pelt. Syrup sacs communicated with their digestive apparatus, wires led to motor nodes in the rudimentary brain. The muscles were clamped to rocker arms which actuated rotors and drive-wheels. The power-wagons, economical, long-lived and docile, were principally used for heavy cartage, earth-moving, heavy tillage and other arduous jobs.

Xanten nodded in profound satisfaction and returned to the power-wagon he had reserved for his own use. Mounting to the seat, he waited. No Meks issued from the barracks. Apparently they were deserted, with the entire crew busy at the hangars. Still, hopefully, the syrup stocks had been destroyed, and many might perish by starvation.

From the direction of the hangars came a single Mek, evidently attracted by the sounds of destruction. Xanten crouched on the seat, and as it passed, coiled his whip around the stocky neck. He heaved; the Mek spun to the ground.

Xanten leaped down, seized its pellet gun. Here was another of the larger Meks, and now Xanten saw it to be without a syrup sac, a Mek in the original state. Astounding! How did the creature survive? Suddenly there were many new questions to be asked—hopefully a few to be answered. Standing on the creature's head, Xanten hacked away the long antenna quills which protruded from the back of the Mek's scalp. It was now insulated, alone, on its own resources—a situation to reduce the most stalwart Mek to apathy.

"Up!" ordered Xanten. "Into the back of the wagon!" He cracked the whip for emphasis.

The Mek at first seemed disposed to defy him, but after a blow or two obeyed. Xanten climbed into the seat and started the power-wagon, directed it to the north. The Birds would be unable to carry both himself and the Mek—or in any event they would cry and complain so raucously that they might as well be believed at first. They might or might not wait until the specified hour of tomorrow's sunset; as likely as not they would sleep the night in a tree, awake in a surly mood and return at once to Castle Hagedorn.

All through the night the power-wagon trundled, with Xanten on the seat and his captive huddled in the rear.

III

1.

The gentlefolk of the castles, for all their assurance, disliked to wander the countryside by night, by reason of what some derided as superstitious fear. Others cited travelers benighted beside moldering ruins and their subsequent visions: the eldritch music they had heard, or the whimper of moonmirkins, or the far horns of spectral huntsmen. Others had seen pale lavender and green lights, and wraiths which ran with long strides through the forest; and Hode Abbey, now a dank tumble, was notorious for the White Hag and the alarming toll she exacted.

A hundred such cases were known, and while the hardheaded scoffed, none needlessly traveled the countryside by night. Indeed, if ghosts truly haunt the scenes of tragedy and heartbreak, then the landscape of Old Earth must be home to ghosts and specters beyond all numbering—especially that region across which Xanten rolled in the power-wagon, where every rock, every meadow, every vale and swale was crusted thick with human experience.

The moon rose high; the wagon trundled

north along an ancient road, the cracked concrete slabs shining pale in the moonlight. Twice Xanten saw flickering orange lights off to the side, and once, standing in the shade of a cypress tree, he thought he saw a tall quiet shape, silently watching him pass. The captive Mek sat plotting mischief, Xanten well knew. Without its quills it must feel depersonified, bewildered, but Xanten told himself that it would not do to doze.

The road led through a town, certain structures of which still stood. Not even the Nomads took refuge in these old towns, fearing either miasma or perhaps the redolence of grief.

The moon reached the zenith. The landscape spread away in a hundred tones of silver, black and gray. Looking about, Xanten thought that for all the notable pleasures of civilized life, there was yet something to be said for the spaciousness and simplicity of Nomadland. The Mek made a stealthy movement. Xanten did not so much as turn his head. He cracked his whip in the air. The Mek became quiet.

All through the night the power-wagon rolled along the old road, with the moon sinking into the west. The eastern horizon glowed green and lemon-yellow, and presently, as the pallid moon disappeared, the sun rose over the distant line of mountains. At this moment, off to the right, Xanten spied a drift of smoke.

He halted the wagon. Standing up on the seat, he craned his neck to spy a Nomad encampment about a quarter-mile distant. He could distinguish three or four dozen tents of various sizes and a dozen dilapidated power-wagons. On the hetman's tall tent he thought he saw a black ideogram that he recognized. If so, this would be the tribe which not long before had trespassed on the Hagedorn domain, and which O.Z. Garr had repulsed.

Xanten settled himself upon the seat, composed his garments, set the power-wagon in motion and guided it toward the camp.

A hundred black-cloaked men, tall and lean as ferrets, watched his approach. A dozen sprang forward, and whipping arrows to bows, aimed them at his heart. Xanten turned them a glance of supercilious inquiry, drove the wagon up to the hetman's tent, halted. He rose to his feet. "Hetman," he called. "Are you awake?"

The hetman parted the canvas which closed off his tent, peered out and after a moment came forth. Like the others he wore a garment of limp black cloth, swathing head and body alike. His face thrust through a square opening: narrow blue eyes, a grotesquely long nose, a chin long, skewed and sharp.

Xanten gave him a curt nod. "Observe this." He jerked his thumb toward the Mek in the back of the wagon. The hetman flicked aside his eyes, studied the Mek a tenth-second and returned to a scrutiny of Xanten. "His kind have revolted against the gentlemen," said Xanten. "In fact they massacre all the men of Earth. Hence, we of Castle Hagedorn make this offer to the Nomads. Come to Castle Hagedorn. We will feed, clothe and arm you. We will train you to discipline and the arts of formal warfare. We will provide the most expert leadership within our power. We will then annihilate the Meks, expunge them from Earth. After the campaign, we will train you to technical skills, and you may pursue profitable and interesting careers in the service of the castles."

The hetman made no reply for a moment. Then his weathered face split into a ferocious grin. He spoke in a voice which Xanten found surprisingly well modulated. "So your beasts have finally risen up to rend you! A pity they forbore so long! Well, it is all one to us. You are both alien folk and sooner or later your bones must bleach together."

Xanten pretended incomprehension. "If I understand you aright, you assert that in the face of alien assault, all men must fight a common battle; and then, after the victory, cooperate still to their mutual advantage. Am I correct?"

The hetman's grin never wavered. "You are not men. Only we of Earth soil and Earth water are men. You and your weird slaves are strangers together. We wish you success in your mutual slaughter."

"Well, then," declared Xanten, "I heard you aright after all: Appeals to your loyalty are ineffectual, so much is clear. What of self-interest, then? The Meks, failing to expunge the gentlefolk of the castles, will turn upon the Nomads and kill them as if they were so many ants."

"If they attack us, we will war on them," said the hetman. "Otherwise let them do as they will."

Xanten glanced thoughtfully at the sky. "We might be willing, even now, to accept a contingent of Nomads into the service of Castle Hagedorn, this to form a cadre from which a larger, more versatile group may be formed."

From the side, another Nomad called in an offensively jeering voice, "You will sew a sac on our backs where you can pour your syrup, hey?"

Xanten replied in an even voice, "The syrup is highly nutritious and supplies all bodily needs."

"Why, then, do you not consume it yourself?"

Xanten disdained reply.

The hetman spoke. "If you wish to supply us weapons, we will take them, and use them against whomever threatens us. But do not expect us to defend you. If you fear for your lives, desert your castles and become Nomads."

"Fear for our lives?" exclaimed Xanten. "What nonsense! Never! Castle Hagedorn is impregnable, as is Janeil, and most of the other castles as well."

The hetman shook his head. "Any time we choose we could take Hagedorn, and kill all you popinjays in your sleep."

"What!" cried Xanten in outrage. "Are you serious?"

"Certainly. On a black night we would send

a man aloft on a great kite and drop him down on the parapets. He would lower a line, haul up ladders and in fifteen minutes the castle is taken."

Xanten pulled at his chin. "Ingenious, but impractical. The Birds would detect such a kite. Or the wind would fail at a critical moment. . . . All this is beside the point. The Meks fly no kites. They plan to make a display against Janeil and Hagedorn, then, in their frustration, go forth and hunt Nomads."

The hetman moved back a step. "What then? We have survived similar attempts by the men of Hagedorn. Cowards all. Hand to hand, with equal weapons, we would make you eat the dirt like the dogs you are."

Xanten raised his eyebrows in elegant disdain. "I fear that you forget yourself. You address a clan chief of Castle Hagedorn. Only fatigue and boredom restrain me from punishing you with this whip."

"Bah!" said the hetman. He crooked a finger to one of his archers. "Split this insolent lordling."

The archer discharged his arrow, but Xanten, who had been expecting some such act, fired his energy-gun, destroying arrow, bow and the archer's hands. He said, "I see I must teach you common respect for your betters; so it means the whip after all." Seizing the hetman by the scalp, he coiled the whip smartly once, twice, thrice around the narrow shoulders. "Let this suffice. I cannot compel you to fight, but at least I can demand decent respect." He leaped to the ground, and seizing the hetman, pitched him into the back of the wagon alongside the Mek. Then, backing the power-wagon around, he departed the camp without so much as a glance over his shoulder, the thwart of the seat protecting his back from arrows.

The hetman scrambled erect, drew his dagger. Xanten turned his head slightly. "Take care! Or I will tie you to the wagon and you shall run behind in the dust."

The hetman hesitated, made a spitting sound between his teeth, drew back. He looked down at his blade, turned it over and sheathed it with a grunt. "Where do you take me?"

Xanten halted the wagon. "No farther. I merely wished to leave your camp with dignity, without dodging and ducking a hail of arrows. You may alight. I take it you still refuse to bring your men into the service of Castle Hagedorn?"

The hetman once more made the spitting sound between his teeth. "When the Meks have destroyed the castles, we shall destroy the Meks, and Earth will be cleared of star-things."

"You are a gang of intractable savages. Very well, alight, return to your encampment. Reflect well before you again show disrespect to a Castle Hagedorn clan chief."

"Bah," muttered the hetman. Leaping down from the wagon, he stalked back down the track toward his camp.

2.

About noon Xanten came to Far Valley, at the edge of the Hagedorn lands. Nearby was a village of Expiationists: malcontents and neurasthenics in the opinion of castle gentlefolk, and a curious group by any standards. A few had held enviable rank; certain others were savants of recognized erudition; but others yet were persons of neither dignity nor reputation, subscribing to the most bizarre and extreme of philosophies. All now performed toil no different from that relegated to the Peasants, and all seemed to take a perverse satisfaction in what—by castle standards—was filth, poverty and degradation.

As might be expected, their creed was by no means homogeneous. Some might better have been described as "nonconformists" or "disassociationists"; another group were "passive expiationists"; and others still, a minority, argued for a dynamic program.

Between castle and village was little intercourse. Occasionally the Expiationists bartered fruit or polished wood for tools, nails, medicaments; or the gentlefolk might make up a party to watch the Expiationists at their dancing and singing. Xanten had visited the village on many such occasions and had been attracted by the artless charm and informality of the folk at their play. Now, passing near the village, Xanten turned aside to follow a lane which wound between tall blackberry hedges and out upon a little common where goats and cattle grazed. Xanten halted the wagon in the shade and saw that the syrup sac was full. He looked back at his captive. "What of you? If you need syrup, pour yourself full. But no, you have no sac. What, then, do you feed upon? Mud? Unsavory fare. I fear none here is rank enough for your taste. Ingest syrup or munch grass, as you will; only do not stray overfar from the wagon, for I watch with an intent eye."

The Mek, sitting hunched in a corner, gave no signal that it comprehended, nor did it move to take advantage of Xanten's offer.

Xanten went to a watering trough and, holding his hands under the trickle which issued from a lead pipe, rinsed his face, then drank a swallow or two from his cupped hand.

Turning, he found that a dozen folk of the village had approached. One he knew well, a man who might have become Godalming, or even Aure, had he not become infected with expiationism.

Xanten performed a polite salute. "A.G. Philidor: it is I, Xanten."

"Xanten, of course. But here I am A.G. Philidor no longer, merely Philidor."

Xanten bowed. "My apologies; I have neglected the full rigor of your informality."

"Spare me your wit," said Philidor. "Why do you bring us a shorn Mek? For adoption, perhaps?" This last alluded to the gentlefolk practice of bringing over-tally babies to the village.

"Now who flaunts his wit? But you have not heard the news?"

"News arrives here last of all. The Nomads are better informed."

"Prepare yourself for surprise. The Meks have revolted against the castles. Halcyon and Delora are demolished, and all killed; perhaps others by this time."

Philidor shook his head. "I am not surprised."

"Well, then, are you not concerned?"

Philidor considered. "To this extent. Our own plans, never very feasible, become more farfetched than ever."

"It appears to me," said Xanten, "that you face grave and immediate danger. The Meks surely intend to wipe out every vestige of humanity. You will not escape."

Philidor shrugged. "Conceivably the danger exists. . . . We will take counsel and decide what to do."

"I can put forward a proposal which you may find attractive," said Xanten. "Our first concern, of course, is to suppress the revolt. There are at least a dozen Expiationist communities, with an aggregate population of two or three thousand—perhaps more. I propose that we recruit and train a corps of highly disciplined troops, supplied from the Castle Hagedorn armory, led by Hagedorn's most expert military theoreticians."

Philidor stared at him incredulously. "You expect us, the Expiationists, to become your soldiers?"

"Why not?" asked Xanten ingenuously. "Your life is at stake no less than ours."

"No one dies more than once."

Xanten in his turn evinced shock. "What? Can this be a former gentleman of Hagedorn speaking? Is this the face a man of pride and courage turns to danger? Is this the lesson of history? Of course not! I need not instruct you in this; you are as knowledgeable as I."

Philidor nodded. "I know that the history of man is not his technical triumphs, his kills, his victories. It is a composite, a mosaic of a trillion pieces, the account of each man's accommodation with his conscience. This is the true history of the race."

Xanten made an airy gesture. "A.G. Philidor, you oversimplify grievously. Do you consider me obtuse? There are many kinds of history. They interact. You emphasize morality. But the ultimate basis of morality is survival. What promotes survival is good; what induces mortifaction is bad."

"Well spoken!" declared Philidor. "But let me propound a parable. May a nation of a million beings destroy a creature who otherwise will infect all with a fatal disease? Yes, you will say. Once more: ten starving beasts hunt you, that they may eat. Will you kill them to save your life? Yes, you will say again, though here you destroy more than you save. Once more: a man inhabits a hut in a lonely valley. A hundred spaceships descend from the sky, and attempt to destroy him. May he destroy these ships in self-defense, even though he is one and they are a hundred thousand? Perhaps you say yes. What, then, if a whole world, a whole race of beings, pits itself against this single man? May he kill all? What if the attackers are as human as himself? What if he were the creature of the first instance, who otherwise will infect a world with disease? You see, there is no area where a simple touchstone avails. We have searched and found none. Hence, at the risk of sinning against Survival, we—I, at least; I can only speak for myself—have chosen a morality which at least allows me calm. I kill—nothing. I destroy—nothing."

"Bah," said Xanten contemptuously. "If a Mek platoon entered this valley and began to kill your children, you would not defend them?"

Philidor compressed his lips, turned away. Another man spoke. "Philidor has defined morality. But who is absolutely moral? Philidor, or I, or you, might desert his morality in such a case."

Philidor said, "Look about you. Is there anyone here you recognize?"

Xanten scanned the group. Nearby stood a girl of extraordinary beauty. She wore a white smock and in the dark hair curling to her shoulders she wore a red flower. Xanten nodded. "I see the maiden O.Z. Garr wished to introduce into his ménage at the castle."

"Exactly," said Philidor. "Do you recall the circumstances?"

"Very well indeed," said Xanten. "There was vigorous objection from the Council of Notables—if for no other reason than the threat to our laws of population control. O.Z. Garr attempted to sidestep the law in this fashion. 'I keep Phanes,' he said. 'At times I maintain as many as six, or even eight, and no one utters a word of protest. I will call this girl Phane and keep her among the rest.' I and others protested. There was almost a duel over this matter. O.Z. Garr was forced to relinquish the girl. She was given into my custody and I conveyed her to Far Valley."

Philidor nodded. "All this is correct. Well—we attempted to dissuade Garr. He refused to be dissuaded, and threatened us with his hunting force of perhaps thirty Meks. We stood aside. Are we moral? Are we strong or weak?"

"Sometimes it is better," said Xanten, "to ignore morality. Even though O.Z. Garr is a gentleman and you are but Expiationists. . . . Likewise in the case of the Meks. They are destroying the castles, and all the men of Earth. If morality means supine acceptance, then morality must be abandoned!"

Philidor gave a sour chuckle. "What a remarkable situation. The Meks are here, likewise Peasants and Birds and Phanes, all altered, transported and enslaved for human pleasure. Indeed, it is this fact that occasions our guilt, for which we must expiate, and now you want us to compound this guilt!"

"It is a mistake to brood overmuch about the past," said Xanten. "Still, if you wish to preserve your option to brood, I suggest that you fight Meks now, or at the very least take refuge in the castle."

"Not I," said Philidor. "Perhaps others may choose to do so."

"You will wait to be killed?"

"No. I and no doubt others will take refuge in the remote mountains."

Xanten clambered back aboard the power-wagon. "If you change your mind, come to Castle Hagedorn."

He departed.

The road continued along the valley, wound up a hillside, crossed a ridge. Far ahead, silhouetted against the sky, stood Castle Hagedorn.

IV

1.

Xanten reported to the council.

"The spaceships cannot be used. The Meks have rendered them inoperative. Any plan to solicit assistance from the Home Worlds is pointless."

"This is sorry news," said Hagedorn with a grimace. "Well, then, so much for that."

Xanten continued. "Returning by power-wagon I encountered a tribe of Nomads. I summoned the hetman and explained to him the advantages of serving Castle Hagedorn. The Nomads, I fear, lack both grace and docility. The hetman gave so surly a response that I departed in disgust.

"At Far Valley I visited the Expiationist village, and made a similar proposal, but with no great success. They are as idealistic as the Nomads are churlish. Both are of a fugitive tendency. The Expiationists spoke of taking refuge in the mountains. The Nomads presumably will retreat into the steppes."

Beaudry snorted. "How will flight help them? Perhaps they gain a few years—but eventually the Meks will find every last one of them; such is their methodicity."

"In the meantime," O.Z. Garr declared peevishly, "we might have organized them into an efficient combat corps, to the benefit of all. Well, then let them perish; we are secure."

"Secure, yes," said Hagedorn gloomily. "But what when the power fails? When the lifts break down? When air circulation cuts off so that we either stifle or freeze? What then?"

O.Z. Garr gave his head a grim shake. "We must steel ourselves to undignified expedients, with as good grace as possible. But the machinery of the castle is sound, and I expect small deterioration or failure for conceivably five or ten years. By that time anything may occur."

Claghorn, who had been leaning indolently back in his seat, spoke at last. "This essentially is a passive program. Like the defection of the Nomads and Expiationists, it looks very little beyond the immediate moment."

O.Z. Garr spoke in a voice carefully polite. "Claghorn is well aware that I yield to none in courteous candor, as well as optimism and directness: in short, the reverse of passivity. But I refuse to dignify a stupid little inconvenience by extending it serious attention. How can he label this procedure passivity? Does the worthy and honorable head of the Claghorns have a proposal which more effectively maintains our status, our standards, our self-respect?"

Claghorn nodded slowly, with a faint half-smile which O.Z. Garr found odiously complacent. "There is a simple and effective method by which the Meks might be defeated."

"Well, then!" cried Hagedorn. "Why hesitate? Let us hear it!"

Claghorn looked around the red velvet-covered table, considering the faces of all: the dispassionate Xanten; Beaudry, burly, rigid, face muscles clenched in an habitual expression unpleasantly like a sneer; old Isseth, as handsome, erect and vital as the most dashing cadet; Hagedorn, troubled, glum, his inward perplexity all too evident; the elegant Garr; Overwhele, thinking savagely of the inconveniences of the future; Aure, toying with his ivory tablet, either bored, morose or defeated; the others displaying various aspects of doubt, foreboding, hauteur, dark resentment, impatience; and in the case of Floy, a quiet smile—or as Isseth later characterized it, an imbecilic smirk—intended to convey his total disassociation from the entire irksome matter.

Claghorn took stock of the faces, and shook his head. "I will not at the moment broach this plan, as I fear it is unworkable. But I must point out that under no circumstances can Castle Hagedorn be as before, even should we survive the Mek attack."

"Bah!" exclaimed Beaudry. "We lose dignity, we become ridiculous, by even so much as discussing the beasts."

Xanten stirred himself. "A distasteful subject, but remember! Halcyon is destroyed, and Delora, and who knows what others? Let us not thrust our heads in the sand! The Meks will not waft away merely because we ignore them."

"In any event," said O.Z. Garr, "Janeil is secure and we are secure. The other folk, unless they are already slaughtered, might do well to visit us during the inconvenience, if they can justify the humiliation of flight to themselves. I myself believe that the Meks will soon come to heel, anxious to return to their posts."

Hagedorn shook his head gloomily. "I find this hard to believe. But very well, then, we shall adjourn."

2.

The radio communication system was the first of the castle's vast array of electrical and mechanical devices to break down. The failure occurred so soon and so decisively that certain of the theoreticians, notably I.K. Harde and Uegus, postulated sabotage by the departing Meks. Others remarked that the system had never been absolutely dependable, that the Meks themselves had been forced to tinker continuously with the circuits, that the failure was simply a result of faulty engineering. I.K. Harde and Uegus inspected the unwieldy apparatus, but the cause of failure was not obvious. After a half hour of consultation they agreed that any attempt to restore the system would necessitate complete redesign and reengineering, with consequent construction of testing and calibration devices, and the fabrication of a complete new family of components. "This is manifestly impossible," stated Uegus in his report to the council. "Even the simplest useful system would require several technician-years. There is not even one single technician to hand. We must therefore await the availability of trained and willing labor."

"In retrospect," stated Isseth, the oldest of the clan chiefs, "it is clear that in many ways we have been less than provident. No matter that the men of the Home Worlds are vulgarians! Men of shrewder calculation than our own would have maintained interworld connection."

"Lack of shrewdness and providence were not the deterring factors," stated Claghorn. "Communication was discouraged simply because the early lords were unwilling that Earth should be overrun with Home-World parvenus. It is as simple as that."

Isseth grunted, and started to make a rejoinder, but Hagedorn said hastily, "Unluckily, as Xanten tells us, the spaceships have been rendered useless, and while certain of our number have a profound knowledge of the theoretical considerations, again who is there to perform the toil? Even were the hangars and spaceships themselves under our control."

O.Z. Garr declared, "Give me six platoons of Peasants and six power-wagons equipped with high-energy cannon, and I'll regain the hangars; no difficulties there!"

Beaudry said, "Well, here's a start, at least. I'll assist in the training of the Peasants, and though I know nothing of cannon operation, rely on me for any advice I can give."

Hagedorn looked around the group, frowned, pulled at his chin. "There are difficulties to this program. First, we have at hand only the single power-wagon in which Xanten returned from his reconnaissance. Then, what of our energy-cannons? Has anyone inspected them? The Meks were entrusted with maintenance, but it is possible, even likely, that they wrought mischief here as well. O.Z. Garr, you are reckoned an expert military theoretician; what can you tell us in this regard?"

"I have made no inspection to date," stated O.Z. Garr. "Today the Display of Antique Tabards will occupy us all until the Hour of Sundown Appraisal[4]." He looked at his watch. "Perhaps now is as good a time as any

4. Display of Antique Tabards; Hour of Sundown Appraisal: the literal sense of the first term was yet relevant; that of the second had become lost and the phrase was a mere formalism, connoting that hour of late afternoon when visits were exchanged, and wines, liqueurs and essences tasted: in short, a time of relaxation and small talk before the more formal convivialities of dining.

to adjourn, until I am able to provide detailed information in regard to the cannons."

Hagedorn nodded his heavy head. "The time indeed grows late. Your Phanes appear today?"

"Only two," replied O.Z. Garr. "The Lazule and the Eleventh Mystery. I can find nothing suitable for the Gossamer Delights nor my little Blue Fay, and the Gloriana still requires tutelage. Today B.Z. Maxelwane's Variflors should repay the most attention."

"Yes," said Hagedorn. "I have heard other remarks to this effect. Very well, then, until tomorrow. Eh, Claghorn, you have something to say?"

"Yes, indeed," Claghorn said mildly. "We have all too little time at our disposal. Best we make the most of it. I seriously doubt the efficacy of Peasant troops; to pit Peasants against Meks is like sending rabbits against wolves. What we need, rather than rabbits, are panthers."

"Ah, yes," Hagedorn said vaguely. "Yes, indeed."

"Where, then, are panthers to be found?" Claghorn looked inquiringly around the table. "Can no one suggest a source? A pity. Well, then, if panthers fail to appear, I suppose rabbits must do. Let us go about the business of converting rabbits into panthers, and instantly. I suggest that we postpone all fetes and spectacles until the shape of our future is more certain."

Hagedorn raised his eyebrows, opened his mouth to speak, closed it again. He looked intently at Claghorn to ascertain whether or not he joked. Then he looked dubiously around the table.

Beaudry gave a rather brassy laugh. "It seems that erudite Claghorn cries panic."

O.Z. Garr stated: "Surely, in all dignity, we cannot allow the impertinence of our servants to cause us such eye-rolling alarm. I am embarrassed even to bring the matter forward."

"I am not embarrassed," said Claghorn, with the full-faced complacence which so exasperated O.Z. Garr. "I see no reason why you should be. Our lives are threatened, in which case a trifle of embarrassment, or anything else, becomes of secondary importance."

O.Z. Garr rose to his feet, performed a brusque salute in Claghorn's direction, of such a nature as to constitute a calculated affront. Claghorn, rising, performed a similar salute, so grave and overly complicated as to invest Garr's insult with burlesque overtones. Xanten, who detested O.Z. Garr, laughed aloud.

O.Z. Garr hesitated, then, sensing that under the circumstances taking the matter further would be regarded as poor form, strode from the chamber.

3.

The Viewing of Antique Tabards, an annual pageant of Phanes wearing sumptuous garments, took place in the Great Rotunda to the north of the central plaza. Possibly half of the gentlemen, but less than a quarter of the ladies, kept Phanes. These were creatures native to the caverns of Albireo Seven's moon: a docile race, both playful and affectionate, which after several thousand years of selective breeding had become sylphs of piquant beauty. Clad in a delicate gauze which issued from pores behind their ears, along their upper arms and down their backs, they were the most inoffensive of creatures, anxious always to please, innocently vain. Most gentlemen regarded them with affection, but rumors sometimes told of ladies drenching an especially hated Phane in tincture of ammonia, which matted her pelt and destroyed her gauze forever.

A gentleman besotted by a Phane was considered a figure of fun. The Phane, though so carefully bred as to seem a delicate girl, if used sexually became crumpled and haggard, with gauzes drooping and discolored, and everyone would know that such and such a gentleman had misused his Phane. In this regard, at least, the women of the castles might exert their superiority, and did so by conducting themselves with such extravagant provocation that the Phanes in contrast seemed the most ingenuous and fragile of nature sprites.

Their life-span was perhaps thirty years, during the last ten of which, after they had lost their beauty, they encased themselves in mantles of gray gauze and performed menial tasks in boudoirs, kitchens, pantries, nurseries and dressing rooms.

The Viewing of Antique Tabards was an occasion more for the viewing of Phanes than the tabards, though these, woven of Phane-gauze, were of great intrinsic beauty in themselves.

The Phane owners sat in a lower tier, tense with hope and pride, exulting when one made an especially splendid display, plunging into black depths when the ritual postures were performed with other than grace and elegance. During each display, highly formal music was plucked from a lute by a gentleman from a clan different to that of the Phane owner, the owner never playing the lute to the performance of his own Phane. The display was never overtly a competition and no formal acclamation was allowed, but all watching made up their minds as to which was the most entrancing and graceful of the Phanes, and the repute of the owner was thereby exalted.

The current Viewing was delayed almost half an hour by reason of the defection of the Meks, and certain hasty improvisations had been necessary. But the gentlefolk of Castle Hagedorn were in no mood to be critical and took no heed of the occasional lapses as a dozen young Peasant bucks struggled to perform unfamiliar tasks. The Phanes were as entrancing as ever, bending, twisting, swaying to plangent chords of the lute, fluttering their fingers as if feeling for raindrops, crouching suddenly and gliding, then springing upright as straight as wands, finally bowing and skipping from the platform.

Halfway through the program a Peasant sidled awkwardly into the Rotunda, and mumbled in an urgent manner to the cadet who came to inquire his business. The cadet at once made his way to Hagedorn's polished jet booth. Hagedorn listened, nodded, spoke a few terse words and settled calmly back in his seat as if the message had been of no consequence, and the gentlefolk of the audience were reassured.

The entertainment proceeded. O.Z. Garr's delectable pair made a fine show, but it was generally felt that Lirlin, a young Phane belonging to Isseth Floy Gazuneth, for the first time at a formal showing, made the most captivating display.

The Phanes appeared for a last time, moving all together through a half-improvised minuet, then performing a final half gay, half regretful salute, departed the Rotunda. For a few moments more the gentlemen and ladies would remain in their booths, sipping essences, discussing the display, arranging affairs and assignations. Hagedorn sat frowning, twisting his hands. Suddenly he rose to his feet. The Rotunda instantly became silent.

"I dislike intruding an unhappy note at so pleasant an occasion," said Hagedorn. "But the news has just been given to me, and it is fitting that all should know. Janeil Castle is under attack. The Meks are there in great force, with hundreds of power-wagons. They have circled the castle with a dike which prevents any effective use of the Janeil energy-cannon.

"There is no immediate danger to Janeil, and it is difficult to comprehend what the Meks hope to achieve, the Janeil walls being all of two hundred feet high.

"The news, nevertheless, is somber, and it means that eventually we must expect a similar investment—though it is even more difficult to comprehend how Meks could hope to inconvenience us. Our water derives from four wells sunk deep into the earth. We have great stocks of food. Our energy is derived from the sun. If necessary, we could condense water and synthesize food from the air—at least I have been so assured by our great biochemical theoretician, X.B. Ladisname. Still—this is the news. Make of it what you will. Tomorrow the Council of Notables will meet."

V

1.

"Well, then," said Hagedorn to the council, "for once let us dispense with formality. O.Z. Garr: what of our cannon?"

O.Z. Garr, wearing the magnificent gray and green uniform of the Overwhele Dragoons, carefully placed his morion on the table, so that the panache stood erect. "Of twelve cannon, four appear to be functioning correctly. Four have been sabotaged by excision of the power-leads. Four have been sabotaged by some means undetectable to careful investigation. I have commandeered a half dozen Peasants who demonstrate a modicum of mechanical ability, and have instructed them in detail. They are currently engaged in splicing the leads. This is the extent of my current information in regard to the cannon."

"Moderately good news," said Hagedorn. "What of the proposed corps of armed Peasants?"

"The project is now under way. A.F. Mull and I.A. Berzelius are now inspecting Peasants with a view to recruitment and training. I can make no sanguine projection as to the military effectiveness of such a corps, even if trained and led by such as A.F. Mull, I.A. Berzelius and myself. The Peasants are a mild, ineffectual race, admirably suited to the grubbing of weeds, but with no stomach whatever for fighting."

Hagedorn glanced around the council. "Are there any other suggestions?"

Beaudry spoke in a harsh, angry voice. "Had the villains but left us our power-wagons, we might have mounted the cannon aboard—the Peasants are equal to this, at least. Then we could roll to Janeil and blast the dogs from the rear."

"These Meks seem utter fiends!" declared Aure. "What conceivably do they have in mind? Why, after all these centuries, must they suddenly go mad?"

"We all ask ourselves the same question," said Hagedorn. "Xanten, you returned from reconnaissance with a captive. Have you attempted to question him?"

"No," said Xanten. "Truth to tell, I haven't thought of him since."

"Why not attempt to question him? Perhaps he can provide a clue or two."

Xanten nodded assent. "I can try. Candidly, I expect to learn nothing."

"Claghorn, you are the Mek expert," said Beaudry. "Would you have thought the creatures capable of so intricate a plot? What do they hope to gain? Our castles?"

"They are certainly capable of precise and meticulous planning," said Claghorn. "Their ruthlessness surprises me—more, possibly, than it should. I have never known them to covet our material possessions, and they show no tendency toward what we consider the concomitants of civilization: fine discriminations of sensation and the like. I have often speculated—I won't dignify the conceit with the status of a theory—that the structural logic of a brain is of rather more consequence than we reckon with. Our own brains are remarkable for their utter lack of rational structure. Considering the haphazard manner in which our thoughts are formed, registered, indexed and recalled, any single rational act becomes a miracle. Perhaps we are incapable of rationality; perhaps all thought is a set of impulses generated by one emotion, monitored by another, ratified by a third. In contrast, the Mek brain is a marvel of what seems to be careful engineering. It is roughly cubical and consists of microscopic cells interconnected by organic fibrils, each a monofilament molecule of negligible electrical resistance. Within each cell is a film of silica, a fluid of variable conductivity and dielectric properties, a cusp of a complex mixture of metallic oxides. The brain is capable of storing great quantities of information in an orderly pattern. No fact is lost, unless it is purposely forgotten, a capacity which the Meks possess. The brain also functions as a radio transceiver, possibly as a radar transmitter and detector, though this again is speculation.

"Where the Mek brain falls short is in its lack of emotional color. One Mek is precisely like another, without any personality differentiation perceptible to us. This, clearly, is a function of their communicative system: unthinkable for a unique personality to develop under these conditions. They served us efficiently and—so we thought—loyally, because they felt nothing about their condition, neither pride in achievement, nor resentment, nor shame. Nothing whatever. They neither loved us nor hated us, nor do they now. It is hard for us to conceive this emotional vacuum, when each of us feels something about everything. We live in a welter of emotions. They are as devoid of emotion as an ice cube. They were fed, housed and maintained in a manner they found satisfactory. Why did they revolt? I have speculated at length, but the single reason which I can formulate seems so grotesque and unreasonable that I refuse to take it seriously. If this after all is the correct explanation. . . ." His voice drifted away.

"Well?" demanded O.Z. Garr peremptorily. "What, then?"

"Then—it is all the same. They are committed to the destruction of the human race. My speculation alters nothing."

Hagedorn turned to Xanten. "All this should assist you in your inquiries."

"I was about to suggest that Claghorn assist me, if he is so inclined," said Xanten.

"As you like," said Claghorn, "though in my opinion the information, no matter what, is irrelevant. Our single concern should be a means to repel them and to save our lives."

"And—except the force of 'panthers' you

mentioned at our previous session—you can conceive of no subtle weapon?" asked Hagedorn wistfully. "A device to set up electrical resonances in their brains, or something similar?"

"Not feasible," said Claghorn. "Certain organs in the creatures' brains function as overload switches. Though it is true that during this time they might not be able to communicate." After a moment's reflection he added thoughtfully, "Who knows? A.G. Bernal and Uegus are theoreticians with a profound knowledge of such projections. Perhaps they might construct such a device, or several, against a possible need."

Hagedorn nodded dubiously, and looked toward Uegus. "Is this possible?"

Uegus frowned. " 'Construct'? I can certainly design such an instrument. But the components—where? Scattered through the storerooms helter-skelter, some functioning, others not. To achieve anything meaningful I must become no better than an apprentice, a Mek." He became incensed, and his voice hardened. "I find it hard to believe that I should be forced to point out this fact. Do you hold me and my talents, then, of such small worth?"

Hagedorn hastened to reassure him. "Of course not! I for one would never think of impugning your dignity."

"Never!" agreed Claghorn. "Nevertheless, during this present emergency, we will find indignities imposed upon us by events, unless now we impose them upon ourselves."

"Very well," said Uegus, a humorless smile trembling at his lips. "You shall come with me to the storeroom. I will point out the components to be brought forth and assembled; you shall perform the toil. What do you say to that?"

"I say yes, gladly, if it will be of real utility. However, I can hardly perform the labor for a dozen different theoreticians. Will any others serve besides myself?"

No one responded. Silence was absolute, as if every gentleman present held his breath.

Hagedorn started to speak, but Claghorn interrupted. "Pardon, Hagedorn, but here, finally, we are stuck upon a basic principle, and it must be settled now."

Hagedorn looked desperately around the council. "Has anyone relevant comment?"

"Claghorn must do as his innate nature compels," declared O.Z. Garr in the silkiest of voices. "I cannot dictate to him. As for myself, I can never demean my status as a gentleman of Hagedorn. This creed is as natural to me as drawing breath; if ever it is compromised I become a travesty of a gentleman, a grotesque mask of myself. This is Castle Hagedorn, and we represent the culmination of human civilization. Any compromise therefore becomes degradation; any expedient diminution of our standards becomes dishonor. I have heard the word 'emergency' used. What a deplorable sentiment! To dignify the ratlike snappings and gnashings of such as the Meks with the word 'emergency' is to my mind unworthy of a gentleman of Hagedorn!"

A murmur of approval went around the council table.

Claghorn leaned far back in his seat, chin on his chest, as if in relaxation. His clear blue eyes went from face to face, then returned to O.Z. Garr whom he studied with dispassionate interest. "Obviously you direct your words to me," he said, "and I appreciate their malice. But this is a small matter." He looked away from O.Z. Garr, to stare up at the massive diamond and emerald chandelier. "More important is the fact that the council as a whole, in spite of my earnest persuasion, seems to endorse your viewpoint. I can urge, expostulate, insinuate no longer, and I will not leave Castle Hagedorn. I find the atmosphere stifling. I trust that you survive the attack of the Meks, though I doubt that you will. They are a clever, resourceful race, untroubled by qualms or preconceptions, and we have long underestimated their quality."

Claghorn rose from his seat, inserted the ivory tablet into its socket. "I bid you all farewell."

Hagedorn hastily jumped to his feet and held forth his arms imploringly. "Do not depart in anger, Claghorn! Reconsider! We need your wisdom, your expertise!"

"Assuredly you do," said Claghorn. "But even more, you need to act upon the advice I have already extended. Until then, we have no common ground, and any further interchange is futile and tiresome." He made a brief, all-inclusive salute and departed the chamber.

Hagedorn slowly resumed his seat. The others made uneasy motions, coughed, looked up at the chandelier, studied their ivory tablets. O.Z. Garr muttered something to B.F. Wyas who sat beside him, who nodded solemnly. Hagedorn spoke in a subdued voice. "We will miss the presence of Claghorn, his penetrating if unorthodox insights. . . . We have accomplished little. Uegus, perhaps you will give thought to the projector under discussion. Xanten, you were to question the captive Mek. O.Z. Garr, you undoubtedly will see to the repair of the energy-cannon. . . . Aside from these small matters, it appears that we have evolved no general plan of action, to help either ourselves or Janeil."

Marune spoke. "What of the other castles? Are they still extant? We have had no news. I suggest that we send Birds to each castle, to learn their condition."

Hagedorn nodded. "Yes, this is a wise motion. Perhaps you will see to this, Marune?"

"I will do so."

"Good. We will now adjourn."

2.

The Birds dispatched by Marune of Aure, one by one returned. Their reports were similar:

"Sea Island is deserted. Marble columns are tumbling along the beach. Pearl Dome is collapsed. Corpses float in the Water Garden."

"Maraval reeks of death. Gentlemen, Peasants, Phanes—all dead. Alas! Even the Birds have departed!"

"Delora: *a ros ros ros*! A dismal scene! No sign of life!"

"Alume is desolate. The great wooden door is smashed. The Green Flame is extinguished."

"There is nothing at Halcyon. The Peasants were driven into a pit."

"Tuang: silence."

"Morninglight: death."

VI

1.

Three days later, Xanten constrained six Birds to a lift-chair, directed them first on a wide sweep around the castle, then south to Far Valley.

The Birds aired their usual complaints, then bounded down the deck in great ungainly hops which threatened to throw Xanten immediately to the pavement. At last gaining the air, they flew up in a spiral; Castle Hagedorn became an intricate miniature far below, each House marked by its unique cluster of turrets and aeries, its own eccentric roof line, its long streaming pennon.

The Birds performed the prescribed circle, skimming the crags and spires of North Ridge; then, setting wings aslant the upstream, they coasted away toward Far Valley.

Over the pleasant Hagedorn domain flew the Birds and Xanten: over orchards, fields, vineyards, Peasant villages. They crossed Lake Maude with its pavilions and docks, the meadows beyond where the Hagedorn cattle and sheep grazed, and presently came to Far Valley, at the limit of Hagedorn lands.

Xanten indicated where he wished to alight; the Birds, who would have preferred a site closer to the village where they could have watched all that transpired, grumbled and cried out in wrath and set Xanten down so roughly that had he not been alert the shock would have pitched him head over heels.

Xanten alighted without elegance but at least remained on his feet. "Await me here!" he ordered. "Do not stray; attempt no flamboyant tricks among the lift-straps. When I return I wish to see six quiet Birds, in neat formation, lift-straps untwisted and untangled. No bickering, mind you! No loud caterwauling, to attract unfavorable comment! Let all be as I have ordered!"

The Birds sulked, stamped their feet, ducked aside their necks, made insulting comments just under the level of Xanten's hearing. Xanten, turning them a final glare of admonition, walked down the lane which led to the village.

The vines were heavy with ripe blackberries and a number of the girls of the village filled baskets. Among them was the girl O.Z. Garr had thought to preempt for his personal use. As Xanten passed, he halted and performed a courteous salute. "We have met before, if my recollection is correct."

The girl smiled, a half rueful, half whimsical smile. "Your recollection serves you well. We met at Hagedorn, where I was taken a captive. And later, when you conveyed me here, after dark, though I could not see your face." She extended her basket. "Are you hungry? Will you eat?"

Xanten took several berries. In the course of the conversation he learned that the girl's name was Glys Meadowsweet, that her parents were not known to her, but were presumably gentlefolk of Castle Hagedorn who had exceeded their birth tally. Xanten examined her even more carefully than before, but could see resemblance to none of the Hagedorn families. "You might derive from Castle Delora. If there is any family resemblance I can detect, it is to the Cosanzas of Delora—a family noted for the beauty of its ladies."

"You are not married?" she asked artlessly.

"No," said Xanten, and indeed he had dissolved his relationship with Araminta only the day before. "What of you?"

She shook her head. "I would never be gathering blackberries otherwise; it is work reserved for maidens. . . . Why do you come to Far Valley?"

"For two reasons. The first to see you." Xanten heard himself say this with surprise. But it was true, he realized with another small shock of surprise. "I have never spoken with you properly and I have always wondered if you were as charming and gay as you are beautiful."

The girl shrugged and Xanten could not be sure whether she was pleased or not, compliments from gentlemen sometimes setting the stage for a sorry aftermath. "Well, no matter. I came also to speak to Claghorn."

"He is yonder," she said in a voice toneless, even cool, and pointed. "He occupies that cottage." She returned to her blackberry picking. Xanten bowed and proceeded to the cottage the girl had indicated.

Claghorn, wearing loose knee-length breeches of gray homespun, worked with an ax chopping faggots into stove-lengths. At the sight of Xanten he halted his toil, leaned on the ax and mopped his forehead. "Ah, Xanten, I am pleased to see you. How are the folk of Castle Hagedorn?"

"As before. There is little to report, even had I come to bring you news."

"Indeed, indeed?" Claghorn leaned on the ax handle surveying Xanten with a bright blue gaze.

"At our last meeting," went on Xanten, "I agreed to question the captive Mek. After doing so I am distressed that you were not at hand to assist, so that you might have resolved certain ambiguities in the responses."

"Speak on," said Claghorn. "Perhaps I shall be able to do so now."

"After the council meeting I descended immediately to the storeroom where the Mek was confined. It lacked nutriment; I gave it syrup and a pail of water, which it sipped sparingly, then evinced a desire for minced clams. I summoned kitchen help and sent them for this commodity and the Mek ingested several pints. As I have indicated, it was an unusual Mek, standing as tall as myself and lacking a syrup sac. I conveyed it to a different chamber, a storeroom for brown plush furniture, and ordered it to a seat.

"I looked at the Mek and it looked at me. The quills which I removed were growing back; probably it could at last receive from Meks elsewhere. It seemed a superior beast, showing neither obsequiousness nor respect, and answered my questions without hesitation.

"First I remarked: 'The gentlefolk of the castles are astounded by the revolt of the Meks. We had assumed that your life was satisfactory. Were we wrong?'

" 'Evidently.' I am sure that this was the word signaled, though never had I suspected the Meks of dryness or wit of any sort.

" 'Very well, then,' I said. 'In what manner?'

" 'Surely it is obvious,' he said. 'We no longer wished to toil at your behest. We wished to conduct our lives by our own traditional standards.'

"The response surprised me. I was unaware that the Meks possessed standards of any kind, much less traditional standards."

Claghorn nodded. "I have been similarly surprised by the scope of the Mek mentality."

"I reproached the Mek: 'Why kill? Why destroy our lives in order to augment your own?' As soon as I had put the question I realized that it had been unhappily phrased. The Mek, I believe, realized the same; however, in reply he signaled something very rapidly which I believe was: 'We knew we must act with decisiveness. Your own protocol made this necessary. We might have returned to Etamin Nine, but we prefer this world Earth, and will make it our own, with our own great slipways, tubs and basking ramps.'

"This seemed clear enough, but I sensed an adumbration extending yet beyond. I said, 'Comprehensible. But why kill, why destroy? You might have taken yourself to a different region. We could not have molested you.'

" 'Infeasible, by your own thinking. A world is too small for two competing races. You intended to send us back to dismal Etamin Nine.'

" 'Ridiculous!' I said. 'Fantasy, absurdity. Do you take me for a mooncalf?'

" 'No,' the creature insisted. 'Two of Castle Hagedorn's notables were seeking the highest post. One assured us that, if elected, this would become his life's aim.'

" 'A grotesque misunderstanding,' I told him. 'One man, a lunatic, cannot speak for all men!'

" 'No? One Mek speaks for all Meks. We think with one mind. Are not men of a like sort?'

" 'Each thinks for himself. The lunatic who assured you this tomfoolery is an evil man. But at least matters are clear. We do not propose to send you to Etamin Nine. Will you withdraw from Janeil, take yourselves to a far land and leave us in peace?'

" 'No,' he said. 'Affairs have proceeded too far. We will now destroy all men. The truth of the statement is clear: one world is too small for two races.'

" 'Unluckily, then, I must kill you,' I told him. 'Such acts are not to my liking, but, with opportunity, you would kill as many gentlemen as possible.' At this the creature sprang upon me and I killed it with an easier mind than had it sat staring.

"Now you know all. It seems that either you or O.Z. Garr stimulated the cataclysm. O.Z. Garr? Unlikely. Impossible. Hence, you, Claghorn, you! have this weight upon your soul!"

Claghorn frowned down at the ax. "Weight, yes. Guilt, no. Ingenuousness, yes; wickedness, no."

Xanten stood back. "Claghorn, your coolness astounds me! Before, when rancorous folk like O.Z. Garr conceived you a lunatic—"

"Peace, Xanten!" exclaimed Claghorn. "This extravagant breast-beating becomes maladroit. What have I done wrong? My fault is that I tried too much. Failure is tragic, but a phthisic face hanging over the cup of the future is worse. I meant to become Hagedorn, I would have sent the slaves home. I failed, the slaves revolted. So do not speak another word. I am bored with the subject. You cannot imagine how your bulging eyes and your concave spine oppress me."

"Bored you may be," cried Xanten. "You decry my eyes, my spine—but what of the thousands dead?"

"How long would they live in any event? Lives as cheap as fish in the sea. I suggest that you put by your reproaches and devote a similar energy to saving yourself. Do you realize that a means exists? You stare at me blankly. I assure you that what I say is true, but you will never learn the means from me."

"Claghorn," said Xanten, "I flew to this spot intending to blow your arrogant head from your body—" Claghorn, no longer heeding, had returned to his wood-chopping.

"Claghorn!" cried Xanten. "Attend me!"

"Xanten, take your outcries elsewhere, if you please. Remonstrate with your Birds."

Xanten swung on his heel and marched back down the lane. The girls picking berries looked at him questioningly and moved aside. Xanten halted to look up and down the lane. Glys Meadowsweet was nowhere to be seen. In a new fury he continued. He stopped short. On a fallen tree a hundred feet from the Birds sat Glys Meadowsweet, examining a blade of grass as if it had been an astonishing artifact of the past. The Birds, for a marvel, had actually obeyed him and waited in a fair semblance of order.

Xanten looked up toward the heavens, kicked at the turf. He drew a deep breath and approached Glys Meadowsweet. He noted that she had tucked a flower into her long loose hair.

After a second or two she looked up and searched his face. "Why are you so angry?"

Xanten slapped his thigh, then seated himself beside her. " 'Angry'? No. I am out of my mind with frustration. Claghorn is as obstreperous as a sharp rock. He knows how

Castle Hagedorn can be saved but he will not divulge his secret."

Glys Meadowsweet laughed—an easy, merry sound, like nothing Xanten had ever heard at Castle Hagedorn. " 'Secret'? When even I know it?"

"It must be a secret," said Xanten. "He will not tell me."

"Listen. If you fear the Birds will hear, I will whisper." She spoke a few words into his ear.

Perhaps the sweet breath befuddled Xanten's mind. But the explicit essence of the revelation failed to strike home into his consciousness. He made a sound of sour amusement. "No secret there. Only what the prehistoric Scythians termed *bathos.* Dishonor to the gentlemen! Do we dance with the Peasants? Do we serve the Birds essences and discuss with them the sheen of our Phanes?"

" 'Dishonor,' then?" She jumped to her feet. "Then it is also dishonor for you to talk to me, to sit here with me, to make ridiculous suggestions—"

"I made no suggestions!" protested Xanten. "I sit here in all decorum—"

"Too much decorum, too much honor!" With a display of passion which astounded Xanten, Glys Meadowsweet tore the flower from her hair and hurled it to the ground. "There! Hence!"

"No," said Xanten in sudden humility. He bent, picked up the flower, kissed it, replaced it in her hair. "I am not over-honorable. I will try my best." He put his arms on her shoulders, but she held him away.

"Tell me," she inquired with a very mature severity, "do you own any of those peculiar insect-women?"

"I? Phanes? I own no Phanes."

With this, Glys Meadowsweet relaxed and allowed Xanten to embrace her, while the Birds clucked, guffawed and made vulgar scratching sounds with their wings.

VII

1.

The summer waxed warm. On June 30 Janeil and Hagedorn celebrated the Fete of Flowers, even though the dike was rising high around Janeil. Shortly after, Xanten flew six select Birds into Castle Janeil by night, and proposed to the council that the population be evacuated by Bird-lift—as many as possible, as many who wished to leave. The council listened with stony faces and without comment passed on to a consideration of other affairs.

Xanten returned to Castle Hagedorn. Using the most careful methods, speaking only to trusted comrades, Xanten enlisted thirty or forty cadets and gentlemen to his persuasion, though inevitably he could not keep the doctrinal thesis of his program secret.

The first reaction of the traditionalists was mockery and charges of poltroonery. At Xanten's insistence, challenges were neither issued nor accepted by his hot-blooded associates.

On the evening of September 9 Castle Janeil fell. The news was brought to Castle Hagedorn by excited Birds who told the grim tale again and again in voices ever more hysterical.

Hagedorn, now gaunt and weary, automatically called a council meeting; it took note of the gloomy circumstances. "We, then, are the last castle! The Meks cannot conceivably do us harm; they can build dikes around our castle walls for twenty years and only work themselves to distraction. We are secure; but it is a strange and portentous thought to realize that at last, here at Castle Hagedorn, live the last gentlemen of the race!"

Xanten spoke in a voice strained with earnest conviction. "Twenty years—fifty years—what difference to the Meks? Once they surround us, once they deploy, we are trapped. Do you comprehend that now is our last opportunity to escape the great cage that Castle Hagedorn is to become?"

" 'Escape,' Xanten? What a word! For shame!" hooted O.Z. Garr. "Take your wretched band, escape! To steppe or swamp or tundra! Go as you like, with your poltroons, but be good enough to give over these incessant alarms!"

"Garr, I have found conviction since I became a 'poltroon.' Survival is good morality. I have this from the mouth of a noted savant."

"Bah! Such as whom?"

"A.G. Philidor, if you must be informed of every detail."

O.Z. Garr clapped his hand to his forehead. "Do you refer to Philidor, the Expiationist? He is of the most extreme stripe, an Expiationist to out-expiate all the rest! Xanten, be sensible, if you please!"

"There are years ahead for all of us," said Xanten in a wooden voice, "if we free ourselves from the castle."

"But the castle is our life!" declared Hagedorn. "In essence, Xanten, what would we be without the castle? Wild animals? Nomads?"

"We would be alive."

O.Z. Garr gave a snort of disgust and turned away to inspect a wall hanging.

Hagedorn shook his head in doubt and perplexity. Beaudry threw his hands up into the air. "Xanten, you have the effect of unnerving us all. You come in here and inflict this dreadful sense of urgency—but why? In Castle Hagedorn we are as safe as in our mothers' arms. What do we gain by throwing aside all—honor, dignity, comfort, civilized niceties—for no other reason than to slink through the wilderness?"

"Janeil was safe," said Xanten. "Today where is Janeil? Death, mildewed cloth, sour wine. What we gain by *slinking* is the assurance of survival. And I plan much more than simple *slinking*."

"I can conceive of a hundred occasions when death is better than life!" snapped Isseth. "Must I die in dishonor and disgrace? Why may my last years not be passed in dignity?"

Into the room came B.F. Robarth. "Councilmen, the Meks approach Castle Hagedorn."

Hagedorn cast a wild look around the chamber. "Is there a consensus? What must we do?"

Xanten threw up his hands. "Everyone must do as he thinks best! I argue no more: I am done, Hagedorn. Will you adjourn the council so that we may be about our affairs? I to my *slinking*?"

"Council is adjourned," said Hagedorn, and all went to stand on the ramparts.

Up the avenue into the castle trooped Peasants from the surrounding countryside, packets slung over their shoulders. Across the valley, at the edge of Bartholomew Forest, was a clot of power-wagons and an amorphous brown-gold mass: Meks.

Aure pointed west. "Look—there they come, up the Long Swale." He turned, peered east. "And look, there at Bambridge: Meks!"

By common consent, all swung about to scan North Ridge. O.Z. Garr pointed to a quiet line of brown-gold shapes. "There they wait, the vermin! They have penned us in! Well, then, let them wait!" He swung away, rode the lift down to the plaza, and crossed swiftly to Zumbeld House, where he worked the rest of the afternoon with his Gloriana, of whom he expected great things.

2.

The following day the Meks formalized the investment. Around Castle Hagedorn a great circle of Mek activity made itself apparent: sheds, warehouses, barracks. Within this periphery, just beyond the range of the energy-cannon, power-wagons thrust up mounds of dirt.

During the night these mounds lengthened toward the castle, similarly the night after. At last the purpose of the mounds became clear: they were a protective cover above passages or tunnels leading toward the crag on which Castle Hagedorn rested.

The following day several of the mounds reached the base of the crag. Presently a succession of power-wagons loaded with rubble began to flow from the far end. They issued, dumped their loads and once again entered the tunnels.

Eight of these aboveground tunnels had been established. From each trundled endless loads of dirt and rock, gnawed from the crag on which Castle Hagedorn sat. To the gentlefolk who crowded the parapets the meaning of the work at last became clear.

"They make no attempt to bury us," said Hagedorn. "They merely mine out the crag from below us!"

On the sixth day of the siege, a great segment of the hillside shuddered, slumped and a tall pinnacle of rock reaching almost up to the base of the walls collapsed.

"If this continues," muttered Beaudry, "our time will be less than that of Janeil."

"Come, then," called O.Z. Garr, suddenly active. "Let us try our energy-cannon. We'll blast open their wretched tunnels, and then what will the rascals do?" He went to the nearest emplacement and shouted down for Peasants to remove the tarpaulin.

Xanten, who happened to be standing nearby, said, "Allow me to assist you." He jerked away the tarpaulin. "Shoot now, if you will."

O.Z. Garr stared at him uncomprehendingly, then leaped forward and swiveled the great projector about so that it aimed at a mound. He pulled the switch; the air crackled in front of the ringed snout, rippled, flickered with purple sparks. The target area steamed, became black, then dark red, then slumped into an incandescent crater. But the underlying earth, twenty feet in thickness, afforded too much insulation; the molten puddle became white-hot but failed to spread or deepen. The energy-cannon gave a sudden chatter, as electricity short-circuited through corroded insulation. The cannon went dead. O.Z. Garr inspected the mechanism in anger and disappointment; then, with a gesture of repugnance, he turned away. The cannons were clearly of limited effectiveness.

Two hours later, on the east side of the crag, another great sheet of rock collapsed, and just before sunset a similar mass sheered from the western face, where the wall of the castle rose almost in an uninterrupted line from the cliff below.

At midnight Xanten and those of his persuasion, with their children and consorts, departed Castle Hagedorn. Six teams of Birds shuttled from the flight deck to a meadow near Far Valley, and long before dawn had transported the entire group. There were none to bid them farewell.

3.

A week later another section of the east cliff fell away, taking a length of rock-melt buttress with it. At the tunnel mouths the piles of excavated rubble had become alarmingly large.

The terraced south face of the crag was the least disturbed, the most spectacular damage having occurred to east and west. Suddenly, a month after the initial assault, a great section of the terrace slumped forward, leaving an irregular crevasse which interrupted the avenue and hurled down the statues of former notables emplaced at intervals along the avenue's balustrade.

Hagedorn called a council meeting. "Circumstances," he said in a wan attempt at facetiousness, "have not bettered themselves. Our most pessimistic expectations have been exceeded: a dismal situation. I confess that I do not relish the prospect of toppling to my death among all my smashed belongings."

Aure made a desperate gesture. "A similar thought haunts me! Death—what of that? All must die! But when I think of my precious belongings, I become sick. My books trampled! my fragile vases smashed! my tabards ripped! my rugs buried! my Phanes strangled! my heirloom chandeliers flung aside! These are my nightmares."

"Your possessions are no less precious than any others," said Beaudry shortly. "Still, they have no life of their own; when we are gone, who cares what happens to them?"

Marune winced. "A year ago I put down eighteen dozen flasks of prime essence; twelve dozen Green Rain; three each of Balthazar and Faidor. Think of these, if you would contemplate tragedy!"

"Had we only known!" groaned Aure. "I would have—I would have. . . ." His voice trailed away.

O.Z. Garr stamped his foot in impatience. "Let us avoid lamentation at all costs! We had a choice, remember? Xanten beseeched us to flee; now he and his like go skulking and foraging through the north mountains with the Expiationists. We chose to remain, for better or worse and unluckily the worse is occurring. We must accept the fact like gentlemen."

To this the council gave melancholy assent.

Hagedorn brought forth a flask of priceless Rhadamanth, and poured with a prodigality which previously would have been unthinkable. "Since we have no future—to our glorious past!"

That night disturbances were noted here and there around the ring of Mek investment: flames at four separate points, a faint sound of hoarse shouting. On the following day it seemed that the tempo of activity had lessened a trifle.

During the afternoon, however, a vast segment of the east cliff fell away. A moment later, as if after majestic deliberation, the tall east wall split off and toppled, leaving the backs of six great Houses exposed to the open sky.

An hour after sunset a team of Birds settled to the flightdeck. Xanten jumped from the seat. He ran down the circular staircase to the ramparts and came down to the plaza by Hagedorn's palace.

Hagedorn, summoned by a kinsman, came forth to stare at Xanten in surprise. "What do you do here? We expected you to be safely north with the Expiationists!"

"The Expiationists are not safely north," said Xanten. "They have joined the rest of us. We are fighting."

Hagedorn's jaw dropped. "Fighting? The gentlemen are fighting Meks?"

"As vigorously as possible."

Hagedorn shook his head in wonder. "The Expiationists too? I understood that they had planned to flee north."

"Some have done so, including A.G. Philidor. There are factions among the Expiationists just as here. Most are not ten miles distant. The same with the Nomads. Some have taken their power-wagons and fled. The rest kill Meks with fanatic fervor. Last night you saw our work. We fired four storage warehouses, destroyed syrup tanks, killed a hundred or more Meks, as well as a dozen power-wagons. We suffered losses, which hurt us because there are few of us and many Meks. This is why I am here. We need more men. Come fight beside us!"

Hagedorn turned, motioning to the great central plaza. "I will call forth the folk from their Houses. Talk to everyone."

4.

The Birds, complaining bitterly at the unprecedented toil, worked all night, transporting the gentlemen who, sobered by the imminent destruction of Castle Hagedorn, were now willing to abandon all scruples and fight for their lives. The staunch traditionalists still refused to compromise their honor, but Xanten gave them cheerful assurance: "Remain here, then, prowling the castle like so many furtive rats. Take what comfort you can in the fact that you are being protected; the future holds little else for you."

And many who heard him stalked away in disgust.

Xanten turned to Hagedorn. "What of you? Do you come or do you stay?"

Hagedorn heaved a deep sigh, almost a groan. "Castle Hagedorn is at an end. No matter what the eventuality. I come with you."

5.

The situation had suddenly altered. The Meks, established in a loose ring around Castle Hagedorn, had calculated upon no resistance from the countryside and little from the castle. They had established their barracks and syrup depots with thought only for convenience and none for defense; raiding parties, consequently, were able to approach, inflict damage and withdraw before sustaining serious losses of their own. Those Meks posted along North Ridge were harassed almost continuously, and finally were driven down with many losses. The circle around Castle Hagedorn became a cusp; then two days later, after the destruction of five more syrup depots, the Meks drew back even farther. Throwing up earthworks before the two tunnels leading under the south face of the crag, they established a more or less tenable defensive position, but now instead of beleaguering, they became the beleaguered, even though power-wagons of broken rock still issued from the crag.

Within the area thus defended, the Meks concentrated their remaining syrup stocks, tools, weapons, ammunition. The area outside the earthworks was floodlit after dark and guarded by Meks armed with pellet guns, making any frontal assault impractical.

For a day the raiders kept to the shelter of the surrounding orchards, appraising the new situation. Then a new tactic was attempted. Six light carriages were improvised and loaded with bladders of a light inflammable oil, with a fire grenade attached. To each of these carriages ten birds were harnessed, and at midnight sent aloft, with a man for each carriage. Flying high, the Birds then glided down through the darkness over the Mek position, where the fire bombs were dropped. The area instantly seethed with flame. The syrup depot burned; the power-wagons, awakened by the flames, rolled frantically back and forth, crushing Meks and stores, colliding with each other, adding vastly to the terror of the fire. The Meks who survived took shelter in the tunnels. Certain of the floodlights were extinguished, and taking advantage of the confusion, the men attacked the earthworks. After a short, bitter battle, the men killed all the sentinels and took up positions commanding the mouths of the tunnels, which now contained all that remained of the Mek army. It seemed as if the Mek uprising had been put down.

VIII

1.

The flames died. The human warriors—three hundred men from the castle, two hundred Expiationists and about three hundred Nomads—gathered about the tunnel mouth and, during the balance of the night, considered methods to deal with the immured Meks. At sunrise, those men of Castle Hagedorn, whose children and consorts were yet inside, went to bring them forth. With them, upon their return, came a group of castle gentlemen: among them Beaudry, O.Z. Garr, Isseth and Aure. They greeted their onetime peers, Hagedorn, Xanten, Claghorn and others, crisply, but with a certain austere detachment which recognized that loss of prestige incurred by those who fought Meks as if they were equals.

"Now what is to happen?" Beaudry inquired of Hagedorn. "The Meks are trapped but you can't bring them forth. Not impossibly they have syrup stored within for the power-wagons; they may well survive for months."

O.Z. Garr, assessing the situation from the standpoint of a military theoretician, came forward with a plan of action. "Fetch down the cannon—or have your underlings do so—and mount them on power-wagons. When the vermin are sufficiently weak, roll the cannon in and wipe out all but a labor force for the castle: we formerly worked four hundred, and this should suffice."

"Hal!" exclaimed Xanten. "It gives me great pleasure to inform you that this will never be. If any Meks survive they will repair the spaceships and instruct us in their maintenance and we will then transport them and Peasants back to their native worlds."

"How, then, do you expect us to maintain our lives?" demanded Garr coldly.

"You have the syrup generator. Fit yourselves with sacs and drink syrup."

Garr tilted back his head, stared coldly down his nose. "This is your voice, yours alone, and your insolent opinion. Others are to be heard from. Hagedorn—you were once a gentleman. Is this also your philosophy, that civilization should wither?"

"It need not wither," said Hagedorn, "provided that all of us—you as well as we—toil for it. There can be no more slaves. I have become convinced of this."

O.Z. Garr turned on his heel, swept back up the avenue into the castle, followed by the most traditional-minded of his comrades. A few moved aside and talked among themselves in low tones, with one or two black looks for Xanten and Hagedorn.

From the ramparts of the castle came a sudden outcry: "The Meks! They are taking the castle! They swarm up the lower passages! Attack, save us!"

The men below stared up in consternation. Even as they looked, the castle portals swung shut.

"How is this possible?" demanded Hagedorn. "I swear all entered the tunnels!"

"It is only too clear," said Xanten bitterly. "While they undermined, they drove a tunnel up to the lower levels!"

Hagedorn started forward as if he would charge up the crag alone, then halted. "We must drive them out. Unthinkable that they pillage our castle!"

"Unfortunately," said Claghorn, "the walls bar us as effectively as they did the Meks."

"We can send up a force by Bird-car! Once we consolidate, we can hunt them down, exterminate them."

Claghorn shook his head. "They can wait on the ramparts and flight deck and shoot down the Birds as they approach. Even if we secured a foothold there would be great bloodshed: one of us killed for every one of them. And they still outnumber us three or four to one."

Hagedorn groaned. "The thought of them reveling among my possessions, strutting about in my clothes, swilling my essences—it sickens me!"

"Listen!" said Claghorn. From on high they heard the hoarse yells of men, the crackle of energy-cannon. "Some of them, at least, hold out on the ramparts!"

Xanten went to a nearby group of Birds

who were for once awed and subdued by events. "Lift me up above the castle, out of range of the pellets, but where I can see what the Meks do!"

"Care, take care!" croaked one of the Birds. "Ill things occur at the castle."

"Never mind; convey me up, above the ramparts!"

The Birds lifted him, swung in a great circle around the crag and above the castle, sufficiently distant to be safe from the Mek pellet guns. Beside those cannon which yet operated stood thirty men and women. Between the great Houses, the Rotunda and the palace, everywhere the cannon could not be brought to bear, swarmed Meks. The plaza was littered with corpses: gentlemen, ladies and their children—all those who had elected to remain at Castle Hagedorn.

At one of the cannon stood O.Z. Garr. Spying Xanten he gave a shout of hysterical rage, swung up the cannon, fired a bolt. The Birds, screaming, tried to swerve aside, but the bolt smashed two. Birds, car, Xanten fell in a great tangle. By some miracle, the four yet alive caught their balance and a hundred feet from the ground, with a frenzied groaning effort, they slowed their fall, steadied, hovered an instant, sank to the ground. Xanten staggered free of the tangle. Men came running. "Are you safe?" called Claghorn.

"Safe, yes. Frightened as well." Xanten took a deep breath and went to sit on an outcrop of rock.

"What's happening up there?" asked Claghorn.

"All dead," said Xanten, "all but a score. Garr has gone mad. He fired on me."

"Look! Meks on the ramparts!" cried A.L. Morgan.

"There!" cried someone else. "Men! They jump! . . . No, they are flung!"

Some were men, some were Meks whom they had dragged with them; with awful slowness they toppled to their deaths. No more fell. Castle Hagedorn was in the hands of the Meks.

Xanten considered the complex silhouette, at once so familiar and so strange. "They can't hope to hold out. We need only destroy the sun-cells, and they can synthesize no syrup."

"Let us do it now," said Claghorn, "before they think of this and man the cannon! Birds!"

He went off to give the orders, and forty Birds, each clutching two rocks the size of a man's head, flapped up, circled the castle and presently returned to report the sun-cells destroyed.

Xanten said, "All that remains is to seal the tunnel entrances against a sudden eruption, which might catch us off guard—then patience."

"What of the Peasants in the stables—and the Phanes?" asked Hagedorn in a forlorn voice.

Xanten gave his head a slow shake. "He

who was not an Expiationist before must become one now."

Claghorn muttered, "They can survive two months—no more."

But two months passed, and three months, and four months: then one morning the great portals opened and a haggard Mek stumbled forth. He signaled: "Men: we starve. We have maintained your treasures. Give us our lives or we destroy all before we die."

Claghorn responded: "These are our terms. We give you your lives. You must clean the castle, remove and bury the corpses. You must repair the spaceships and teach us all you know regarding them. We will then transport you to Etamin Nine."

2.

Five years later Xanten and Glys Meadowsweet, with their two children, had reason to travel north from their home near Sande River. They took occasion to visit Castle Hagedorn, where now lived only two or three dozen folk, among them Hagedorn.

He had aged, so it seemed to Xanten. His hair was white; his face, once bluff and hearty, had become thin, almost waxen. Xanten could not determine his mood.

They stood in the shade of a walnut tree, with castle and crag looming above them. "This is now a great museum," said Hagedorn. "I am curator, and this will be the function of all the Hagedorns who come after me, for there is incalculable treasure to guard and maintain. Already the feeling of antiquity has come to the castle. The Houses are alive with ghosts. I see them often, especially on the nights of the fetes. . . . Ah, those were the times, were they not, Xanten?"

"Yes, indeed," said Xanten. He touched the heads of his two children. "Still, I have no wish to return to them. We are men now, on our own world, as we never were before."

Hagedorn gave a somewhat regretful assent. He looked up at the vast structure, as if now were the first occasion he had laid eyes on it. "The folk of the future—what will they think of Castle Hagedorn? Its treasures, its books, its tabards?"

"They will come, they will marvel," said Xanten. "Almost as I do today."

"There is much at which to marvel. Will you come within, Xanten? There are still flasks of noble essence laid by."

"Thank you, no," said Xanten. "There is too much to stir old memories. We will go our way, and I think immediately."

Hagedorn nodded sadly. "I understand very

well. I myself am often given to reverie these days. Well then, good-bye, and journey home with pleasure."

"We will do so, Hagedorn. Thank you and good-bye."

Watchful eyes scanned us from slots in the wall. When we were at midpoint in the gate, a fat, pockmarked Sentinel with sagging jowls halted us and asked our business in Roum. I stated my guild and purpose, and he gave a snort of disgust.

"Go elsewhere, Watcher! We need only useful men here."

"Watching has its uses," I said mildly.

"No doubt. No doubt." He squinted at Avluela. "Who's this? Watchers are celibates, no?"

"She is nothing more than a traveling companion."

The Sentinel guffawed coarsely. "It's a route you travel often, I wager! Not that there's much to her." He ran his hands quickly over her, raising an eyebrow as he encountered the mounds of her wings below her shoulders. "What's this? What's this? More in back than in front! A Flier, are you? Very dirty business, Fliers consorting with foul old Watchers." He chuckled and put his hand on Avluela's body in a way that sent Gormon starting forward in a fury, murder in his fire-circled eyes.

ROBERT SILVERBERG

NIGHTWINGS

A TOM DOHERTY ASSOCIATES BOOK
NEW YORK

NIGHTWINGS

A Tor Book
Published by Tom Doherty Associates, Inc.
49 West 24th Street
New York, N.Y. 10010

Cover art by Mark J. Ferrari

ISBN: 0-812-50194-2 Can. ISBN: 0-812-50274-4

First Tor edition: December 1989

Printed in the United States of America

0 9 8 7 6 5 4 3 2 1

1

Roum is a city built on seven hills. They say it was a capital of man in one of the earlier cycles. I did not know of that, for my guild was Watching, not Remembering; but yet as I had my first glimpse of Roum, coming upon it from the south at twilight, I could see that in former days it must have been of great significance. Even now it was a mighty city of many thousands of souls.

Its bony towers stood out sharply against the dusk. Lights glimmered appealingly. On my left hand the sky was ablaze with splendor as the sun relinquished possession; streaming bands of azure and violet and crimson folded and writhed about one another in the nightly dance that brings the darkness. To my right, blackness had already come. I attempted to find the seven hills, and failed, and still I knew that this was that Roum of majesty toward which all roads are bent, and I felt awe and deep respect for the works of our bygone fathers.

We rested by the long straight road, looking up at Roum. I said, "It is a goodly city. We will find employment there."

Beside me, Avluela fluttered her lacy wings. "And food?" she asked in her high, fluty voice. "And shelter? And wine?"

"Those too," I said. "All of those."

"How long have we been walking, Watcher?" she asked.

"Two days. Three nights."

"If I had been flying, it would have been more swift."

"For you," I said. "You would have left us far behind and never seen us again. Is that your desire?"

She came close to me and rubbed the rough fabric of my sleeve, and then she pressed herself at me the way a flirting cat might do. Her wings unfolded into two broad sheets of gossamer through which I could still see the sunset and the evening lights, blurred, distorted, magical. I sensed the fragrance of her midnight hair. I put my arms to her and embraced her slender, boyish body.

She said, "You know it is my desire to remain with you always, Watcher. Always!"

"Yes, Avluela."

"Will we be happy in Roum?"

"We will be happy," I said, and released her.

"Shall we go into Roum now?"

"I think we should wait for Gormon," I said, shaking my head. "He'll be back soon from his explorations." I did not want to tell her of my weariness. She was only a child, seventeen summers old; what did she know of weariness or of age? And I was old. Not as old as Roum, but old enough.

"While we wait," she said, "may I fly?"

"Fly, yes."

I squatted beside our cart and warmed my hands at the throbbing generator while Avluela prepared to fly. First she removed her garments, for her wings have little strength and she cannot lift such extra baggage. Lithely, deftly, she peeled the glassy bubbles from her tiny feet and wriggled free of her crimson jacket and of her soft, furry leggings. The vanishing light in the west sparkled over her slim form. Like all Fliers, she carried no surplus body tissue: her breasts were mere bumps, her buttocks flat, her thighs so spindly that there was a span of inches between them when she stood. Could she have weighed more than a quintal? I doubt it. Looking at her, I felt, as always, gross and earthbound, a thing of loathsome flesh, and yet I am not a heavy man.

By the roadside she genuflected, knuckles to the ground, head bowed to knees, as she said whatever ritual it is that the Fliers say. Her back was to me. Her delicate wings fluttered, filled with life, rose about her like a cloak whipped up by the breeze. I could not comprehend how such wings could possibly lift even so slight a form as Avluela's. They were not hawk-wings but butterfly-wings, veined and transparent, marked here and there with blotches of pigment, ebony and turquoise and scarlet. A sturdy ligament joined them to the two flat pads of muscle beneath her sharp shoulder blades; but what she did not have was the massive breastbone

of a flying creature, the bands of corded muscle needed for flight. Oh, I know that the Fliers use more than muscle to get aloft, that there are mystical disciplines in their mystery. Even so, I, who was of the Watchers, remained skeptical of the more fantastic guilds.

Avluela finished her words. She rose; she caught the breeze with her wings; she ascended several feet. There she remained, suspended between earth and sky, while her wings beat frantically. It was not yet night, and Avluela's wings were merely nightwings. By day she could not fly, for the terrible pressure of the solar wind would hurl her to the ground. Now, midway between dusk and dark, it was still not the best time for her to go up. I saw her thrust toward the east by the remnant of light in the sky. Her arms as well as her wings thrashed; her small pointed face was grim with concentration; on her thin lips were the words of her guild. She doubled her body and shot it out, head going one way, rump the other; and abruptly she hovered horizontally, looking groundward, her wings thrashing against the air. *Up, Avluela! Up!*

Up it was, as by will alone she conquered the vestige of light that still glowed.

With pleasure I surveyed her naked form against the darkness. I could see her clearly, for a Watcher's eyes are keen. She was five times her own height in the air, now, and her wings spread to their full expanse, so that the towers of Roum were in partial eclipse for me. She waved. I threw her a kiss and offered

words of love. Watchers do not marry, nor do they engender children, but yet Avluela was as a daughter to me, and I took pride in her flight. We had traveled together a year, now, since we had first met in Agupt, and it was as though I had known her all my long life. From her I drew a renewal of strength. I do not know what it was she drew from me: security, knowledge, a continuity with the days before her birth. I hoped only that she loved me as I loved her.

Now she was far aloft. She wheeled, soared, dived, pirouetted, danced. Her long black hair streamed from her scalp. Her body seemed only an incidental appendage to those two great wings which glistened and throbbed and gleamed in the night. Up she rose, glorying in her freedom from gravity, making me feel all the more leaden-footed; and like some slender rocket she shot abruptly away in the direction of Roum. I saw the soles of her feet, the tips of her wings; then I saw her no more.

I sighed. I thrust my hands into the pits of my arms to keep them warm. How is it that I felt a winter chill while the girl Avluela could soar joyously bare through the sky?

It was now the twelfth of the twenty hours, and time once again for me to do the Watching. I went to the cart, opened my cases, prepared the instruments. Some of the dial covers were yellowed and faded; the indicator needles had lost their luminous coating; sea stains defaced the instrument housings, a relic of the time that pirates had assailed

me in Earth Ocean. The worn and cracked levers and nodes responded easily to my touch as I entered the preliminaries. First one prays for a pure and perceptive mind; then one creates the affinity with one's instruments; then one does the actual Watching, searching the starry heavens for the enemies of man. Such was my skill and my craft. I grasped handles and knobs, thrust things from my mind, prepared myself to become an extension of my cabinet of devices.

I was only just past my threshold and into the first phase of Watchfulness when a deep and resonant voice behind me said, "Well, Watcher, how goes it?"

I sagged against the cart. There is a physical pain in being wrenched so unexpectedly from one's work. For a moment I felt claws clutching at my heart. My face grew hot; my eyes would not focus; the saliva drained from my throat. As soon as I could, I took the proper protective measures to ease the metabolic drain, and severed myself from my instruments. Hiding my trembling as much as possible, I turned around.

Gormon, the other member of our little band, had appeared and stood jauntily beside me. He was grinning, amused at my distress, but I could not feel angry with him. One does not show anger at a guildless person no matter what the provocation.

Tightly, with effort, I said, "Did you spend your time rewardingly?"

"Very. Where's Avluela?"

I pointed heavenward. Gormon nodded.

"What have you found?" I asked.

"That this city is definitely Roum."

"There never was doubt of that."

"For me there was. But now I have proof."

"Yes?"

"In the overpocket. Look!"

From his tunic he drew his overpocket, set it on the pavement beside me, and expanded it so that he could insert his hands into its mouth. Grunting a little, he began to pull something heavy from the pouch—something of white stone—a long marble column, I now saw, fluted, pocked with age.

"From a temple of Imperial Roum!" Gormon exulted.

"You shouldn't have taken that."

"Wait!" he cried, and reached into the overpocket once more. He took from it a handful of circular metal plaques and scattered them jingling at my feet. "Coins! Money! Look at them, Watcher! The faces of the Caesars!"

"Of whom?"

"The ancient rulers. Don't you know your history of past cycles?"

I peered at him curiously. "You claim to have no guild, Gormon. Could it be you are a Rememberer and are concealing it from me?"

"Look at my face, Watcher. Could I belong to any guild? Would a Changeling be taken?"

"True enough," I said, eyeing the golden hue of him, the thick waxen skin, the red-pupiled eyes, the jagged mouth. Gormon had been weaned on teratogenetic drugs; he was a monster, handsome in his way, but a mon-

ster nevertheless, a Changeling, outside the laws and customs of man as they are practiced in the Third Cycle of civilization. And there is no guild of Changelings.

"There's more," Gormon said. The overpocket was infinitely capacious; the contents of a world, if need be, could be stuffed into its shriveled gray maw, and still it would be no longer than a man's hand. Gormon took from it bits of machinery, reading spools, an angular thing of brown metal that might have been an ancient tool, three squares of shining glass, five slips of paper—*paper*!—and a host of other relics of antiquity. "See?" he said. "A fruitful stroll, Watcher! And not just random booty. Everything recorded, everything labeled, stratum, estimated age, position when *in situ.* Here we have many thousands of years of Roum."

"Should you have taken these things?" I asked doubtfully.

"Why not? Who is to miss them? Who of this cycle cares for the past?"

"The Rememberers."

"They don't need solid objects to help them do their work."

"Why do you want these things, though?"

"The past interests me, Watcher. In my guildless way I have my scholarly pursuits. Is that wrong? May not even a monstrosity seek knowledge?"

"Certainly, certainly. Seek what you wish. Fulfill yourself in your own way. This is Roum. At dawn we enter. I hope to find employment here."

"You may have difficulties."

"How so?"

"There are many Watchers already in Roum, no doubt. There will be little need for your services."

"I'll seek the favor of the Prince of Roum," I said.

"The Prince of Roum is a hard and cold and cruel man."

"You know of him?"

Gormon shrugged. "Somewhat." He began to stuff his artifacts back in the overpocket. "Take your chances with him, Watcher. What other choice do you have?"

"None," I said, and Gormon laughed, and I did not.

He busied himself with his ransacked loot of the past. I found myself deeply depressed by his words. He seemed so sure of himself in an uncertain world, this guildless one, this mutated monster, this man of inhuman look; how could he be so cool, so casual? He lived without concern for calamity and mocked those who admitted to fear. Gormon had been traveling with us for nine days, now, since we had met him in the ancient city beneath the volcano to the south by the edge of the sea. I had not suggested that he join us; he had invited himself along, and at Avluela's bidding I accepted. The roads are dark and cold at this time of year, and dangerous beasts of many species abound, and an old man journeying with a girl might well consider taking with him a brawny one like Gormon. Yet

there were times I wished he had not come with us, and this was one.

Slowly I walked back to my equipment.

Gormon said, as though first realizing it, "Did I interrupt you at your Watching?"

I said mildly, "You did."

"Sorry. Go and start again. I'll leave you in peace." And he gave me his dazzling lopsided smile, so full of charm that it took the curse off the easy arrogance of his words.

I touched the knobs, made contact with the nodes, monitored the dials. But I did not enter Watchfulness, for I remained aware of Gormon's presence and fearful that he would break into my concentration once again at a painful moment, despite his promise. At length I looked away from the apparatus. Gormon stood at the far side of the road, craning his neck for some sight of Avluela. The moment I turned to him he became aware of me.

"Something wrong, Watcher?"

"No. The moment's not propitious for my work. I'll wait."

"Tell me," he said. "When Earth's enemies really do come from the stars, will your machines let you know it?"

"I trust they will."

"And then?"

"Then I notify the Defenders."

"After which your life's work is over?"

"Perhaps," I said.

"Why a whole guild of you, though? Why not one master center where the Watch is

kept? Why a bunch of itinerant Watchers drifting from place to place?"

"The more vectors of detection," I said, "the greater the chance of early awareness of the invasion."

"Then an individual Watcher might well turn his machines on and not see anything, with an invader already here."

"It could happen. And so we practice redundancy."

"You carry it to an extreme, I sometimes think." Gormon laughed. "Do you actually believe an invasion is coming?"

"I do," I said stiffly. "Else my life was a waste."

"And why should the star people want Earth? What do we have here besides the remnants of old empires? What would they do with miserable Roum? With Perris? With Jorslem? Rotting cities! Idiot princes! Come, Watcher, admit it: the invasion's a myth, and you go through meaningless motions four times a day. Eh?"

"It is my craft and my science to Watch. It is yours to jeer. Each of us to our speciality, Gormon."

"Forgive me," he said with mock humility. "Go, then, and Watch."

"I shall."

Angrily I turned back to my cabinet of instruments, determined now to ignore any interruption, no matter how brutal. The stars were out; I gazed at the glowing constellations, and automatically my mind registered

the many worlds. Let us Watch, I thought. Let us keep our vigil despite the mockers.

I entered full Watchfulness.

I clung to the grips and permitted the surge of power to rush through me. I cast my mind to the heavens and searched for hostile entities. What ecstasy! What incredible splendor! I who had never left this small planet roved the black spaces of the void, glided from star to burning star, saw the planets spinning like tops. Faces stared back at me as I journeyed, some without eyes, some with many eyes, all the complexity of the many-peopled galaxy accessible to me. I spied out possible concentrations of inimicable force. I inspected drilling-grounds and military encampments. I sought, as I had sought four times daily for all my adult life, for the invaders who had been promised us, the conquerors who at the end of days were destined to seize our tattered world.

I found nothing, and when I came up from my trance, sweaty and drained, I saw Avluela descending.

Feather-light she landed. Gormon called to her, and she ran, bare, her little breasts quivering, and he enfolded her smallness in his powerful arms, and they embraced, not passionately but joyously. When he released her she turned to me.

"Roum," she gasped. "*Roum!*"

"You saw it?"

"Everything! Thousands of people! Lights! Boulevards! A market! Broken buildings

many cycles old! Oh, Watcher, how wonderful Roum is!"

"Your flight was a good one, then," I said.

"A miracle!"

"Tomorrow we go to dwell in Roum."

"No, Watcher, tonight, tonight!" She was girlishly eager, her face bright with excitement. "It's just a short journey more! Look, it's just over there!"

"We should rest first," I said. "We do not want to arrive weary in Roum."

"We can rest when we get there," Avluela answered. "Come! Pack everything! You've done your Watching, haven't you?"

"Yes. Yes."

"Then let's go. To Roum! To Roum!"

I looked in appeal at Gormon. Night had come; it was time to make camp, to have our few hours of sleep.

For once Gormon sided with me. He said to Avluela, "The Watcher's right. We can all use some rest. We'll go on into Roum at dawn."

Avluela pouted. She looked more like a child than ever. Her wings drooped; her underdeveloped body slumped. Petulantly she closed her wings until they were mere fist-sized humps on her back, and picked up the garments she had scattered on the road. She dressed while we made camp. I distributed food tablets; we entered our receptacles; I fell into troubled sleep and dreamed of Avluela limned against the crumbling moon, and Gormon flying beside her. Two hours before dawn I arose and performed my first Watch of the new day, while they still slept. Then I

aroused them, and we went onward toward the fabled imperial city, onward toward Roum.

2

The morning's light was bright and harsh, as though this were some young world newly created. The road was all but empty; people do not travel much in these latter days unless, like me, they are wanderers by habit and profession. Occasionally we stepped aside to let a chariot of some member of the guild of Masters go by, drawn by a dozen expressionless neuters harnessed in series. Four such vehicles went by in the first two hours of the day, each shuttered and sealed to hide the Master's proud features from the gaze of such common folk as we. Several rollerwagons laden with produce passed us, and a number of floaters soared overhead. Generally we had the road to ourselves, however.

The environs of Roum showed vestiges of antiquity: isolated columns, the fragments of an aqueduct transporting nothing from nowhere to nowhere, the portals of a vanished temple. That was the oldest Roum we saw, but there were accretions of the later Roums

of subsequent cycles: the huts of peasants, the domes of power drains, the hulls of dwelling-towers. Infrequently we met with the burned-out shell of some ancient airship. Gormon examined everything, taking samples from time to time. Avluela looked, wide-eyed, saying nothing. We walked on, until the walls of the city loomed before us.

They were of a blue glossy stone, neatly joined, rising to a height of perhaps eight men. Our road pierced the wall through a corbeled arch; the gate stood open. As we approached the gate, a figure came toward us; he was hooded, masked, a man of extraordinary height wearing the somber garb of the guild of Pilgrims. One does not approach such a person oneself, but one heeds him if he beckons. The Pilgrim beckoned.

Through his speaking grille he said, "Where from?"

"The south. I lived in Agupt awhile, then crossed Land Bridge to Talya," I replied.

"Where bound?"

"Roum, awhile."

"How goes the Watch?"

"As customary."

"You have a place to stay in Roum?" the Pilgrim asked.

I shook my head. "We trust to the kindness of the Will."

"The Will is not always kind," said the Pilgrim absently. "Nor is there much need of Watchers in Roum. Why do you travel with a Flier?"

"For company's sake. And because she is young and needs protection."

"Who is the other one?"

"He is guildless, a Changeling."

"So I can see. But why is he with you?"

"He is strong and I am old, and so we travel together. Where are you bound, Pilgrim?"

"Jorslem. Is there another destination for my guild?"

I conceded the point with a shrug.

The Pilgrim said, "Why do you not come to Jorslem with me?"

"My road lies north now. Jorslem is in the south, close by Agupt."

"You have been to Agupt and not to Jorslem?" he said, puzzled.

"Yes. The time was not ready for me to see Jorslem."

"Come now. We will walk together on the road, Watcher, and we will talk of the old times and of the times to come, and I will assist you in your Watching, and you will assist me in my communions with the Will. Is it agreed?"

It was a temptation. Before my eyes flashed the image of Jorslem the Golden, its holy buildings and shrines, its places of renewal where the old are made young, its spires, its tabernacles. Even though I am a man set in his ways, I was willing at the moment to abandon Roum and go with the Pilgrim to Jorslem.

I said, "And my companions—"

"Leave them. It is forbidden for me to travel with the guildless, and I do not wish to

travel with a female. You and I, Watcher, will go to Jorslem together."

Avluela, who had been standing to one side frowning through all this colloquy, shot me a look of sudden terror.

"I will not abandon them," I said.

"Then I go to Jorslem alone," said the Pilgrim. Out of his robe stretched a bony hand, the fingers long and white and steady. I touched my fingers reverently to the tips of his, and the Pilgrim said, "Let the Will give you mercy, friend Watcher. And when you reach Jorslem, search for me."

He moved on down the road without further conversation.

Gormon said to me, "You would have gone with him, wouldn't you?"

"I considered it."

"What could you find in Jorslem that isn't here? That's a holy city and so is this. Here you can rest awhile. You're in no shape for more walking now."

"You may be right," I conceded, and with the last of my energy I strode toward the gate of Roum.

Watchful eyes scanned us from slots in the wall. When we were at midpoint in the gate, a fat, pockmarked Sentinel with sagging jowls halted us and asked our business in Roum. I stated my guild and purpose, and he gave a snort of disgust.

"Go elsewhere, Watcher! We need only useful men here."

"Watching has its uses," I said mildly.

"No doubt. No doubt." He squinted at Av-

luela. "Who's this? Watchers are celibates, no?"

"She is nothing more than a traveling companion."

The Sentinel guffawed coarsely. "It's a route you travel often, I wager! Not that there's much to her. What is she, thirteen, fourteen? Come here, child. Let me check you for contraband." He ran his hands quickly over her, scowling as he felt her breasts, then raising an eyebrow as he encountered the mounds of her wings below her shoulders. "What's this? What's this? More in back than in front! A Flier, are you? Very dirty business, Fliers consorting with foul old Watchers." He chuckled and put his hand on Avluela's body in a way that sent Gormon starting forward in fury, murder in his fire-circled eyes. I caught him in time and grasped his wrist with all my strength, holding him back lest he ruin the three of us by an attack on the Sentinel. He tugged at me, nearly pulling me over; then he grew calm and subsided, icily watching as the fat one finished checking Avluela for "contraband."

At length the Sentinel turned in distaste to Gormon and said, "What kind of thing are you?"

"Guildless, your mercy," Gormon said in sharp tones. "The humble and worthless product of teratogenesis, and yet nevertheless a free man who desires entry to Roum."

"Do we need more monsters here?"

"I eat little and work hard."

"You'd work harder still, if you were neutered," said the Sentinel.

Gormon glowered. I said, "May we have entry?"

"A moment." The Sentinel donned his thinking cap and narrowed his eyes as he transmitted a message to the memory tanks. His face tensed with the effort; then it went slack, and moments later came the reply. We could not hear the transaction at all; but from his disappointed look, it appeared evident that no reason had been found to refuse us admission to Roum.

"Go on in," he said. "The three of you. Quickly!"

We passed beyond the gate.

Gormon said, "I could have split him open with a blow."

"And be neutered by nightfall. A little patience, and we've come into Roum."

"The way he handled her—!"

"You take a very possessive attitude toward Avluela," I said. "Remember that she's a Flier, and not sexually available to the guildless."

Gormon ignored my thrust. "She arouses me no more than you do, Watcher. But it pains me to see her treated that way. I would have killed him if you hadn't held me back."

Avluela said, "Where shall we stay, now that we're in Roum?"

"First let me find the headquarters of my guild," I said. "I'll register at the Watchers' Inn. After that, perhaps we'll hunt up the Fliers' Lodge for a meal."

"And then," said Gormon drily, "we'll go to the Guildless Gutter and beg for coppers."

"I pity you because you are a Changeling," I told him, "but I find it ungraceful of you to pity yourself. Come."

We walked up a cobbled, winding street away from the gate and into Roum itself. We were in the outer ring of the city, a residential section of low, squat houses topped by the unwieldy bulk of defense installations. Within lay the shining towers we had seen from the fields the night before; the remnant of ancient Roum carefully preserved across ten thousand years or more; the market, the factory zone, the communications hump, the temples of the Will, the memory tanks, the sleepers' refuges, the outworlders' brothels, the government buildings, the headquarters of the various guilds.

At the corner, beside a Second Cycle building with walls of rubbery texture, I found a public thinking cap and slipped it on my forehead. At once my thoughts raced down the conduit until they came to the interface that gave them access to one of the storage brains of a memory tank. I pierced the interface and saw the wrinkled brain itself, pale gray against the deep green of its housing. A Rememberer once told me that, in cycles past, men built machines to do their thinking for them, although these machines were hellishly expensive and required vast amounts of space and drank power gluttonously. That was not the worst of our forefathers' follies; but why build artificial brains when death

each day liberates scores of splendid natural ones to hook into the memory tanks? Was it that they lacked the knowledge to use them? I find that hard to believe.

I gave the brain my guild identification and asked the coordinates of our inn. Instantly I received them, and we set out, Avluela on one side of me, Gormon on the other, myself wheeling, as always, the cart in which my instruments resided.

The city was crowded. I had not seen such throngs in sleepy, heat-fevered Agupt, nor at any other point on my northward journey. The streets were full of Pilgrims, secretive and masked. Jostling through them went busy Rememberers and glum Merchants and now and then the litter of a Master. Avluela saw a number of Fliers, but was barred by the tenets of her guild from greeting them until she had undergone her ritual purification. I regret to say that I spied many Watchers, all of whom looked upon me disdainfully and without welcome. I noted a good many Defenders and ample representation of such lesser guilds as Vendors, Servitors, Manufactories, Scribes, Communicants, and Transporters. Naturally, a host of neuters went silently about their humble business, and numerous outworlders of all descriptions flocked the streets, most of them probably tourists, some here to do what business could be done with the sullen, poverty-blighted people of Earth. I noticed many Changelings limping furtively through the crowd, not one of them as proud of bearing as Gormon be-

side me. He was unique among his kind; the others, dappled and piebald and asymmetrical, limbless or overlimbed, deformed in a thousand imaginative and artistic ways, were slinkers, squinters, shufflers, hissers, creepers; they were cutpurses, brain-drainers, organ-peddlers, repentance-mongers, gleam-buyers, but none held himself upright as though he thought he were a man.

The guidance of the brain was exact, and in less than an hour of walking we arrived at the Watchers' Inn. I left Gormon and Avluela outside and wheeled my cart within.

Perhaps a dozen members of my guild lounged in the main hall. I gave them the customary sign, and they returned it languidly. Were these the guardians on whom Earth's safety depended? Simpletons and weaklings!

"Where may I register?" I asked.

"New? Where from?"

"Agupt was my last place of registry."

"Should have stayed there. No need of Watchers here."

"Where may I register?" I asked again.

A foppish youngster indicated a screen in the rear of the great room. I went to it, pressed my fingertips against it, was interrogated, and gave my name, which a Watcher may utter only to another Watcher and only within the precincts of an inn. A panel shot open, and a puffy-eyed man who wore the Watcher emblem on his right cheek and not on the left, signifying his high rank in the guild, spoke my name and said, "You should

have known better than to come to Roum. We're over our quota."

"I claim lodging and employment nonetheless."

"A man with your sense of humor should have been born into the Guild of Clowns," he said.

"I see no joke."

"Under laws promulgated by our guild in the most recent session, an inn is under no obligation to take new lodgers once it has reached its assigned capacity. We are at our assigned capacity. Farewell, my friend."

I was aghast. "I know of no such regulation! This is incredible! For a guild to turn away a member from its own inn—when he arrives footsore and numb! A man of my age, having crossed Land Bridge out of Agupt, here as a stranger and hungry in Roum—"

"Why did you not check with us first?"

"I had no idea it would be necessary."

"The new regulations—"

"May the Will shrivel the new regulations!" I shouted. "I demand lodging! To turn away one who has Watched since before you were born—"

"Easy, brother, easy."

"Surely you have some corner where I can sleep—some crumbs to let me eat—"

Even as my tone had changed from bluster to supplication, his expression softened from indifference to mere disdain. "We have no room. We have no food. These are hard times for our guild, you know. There is talk that we will be disbanded altogether, as a useless lux-

ury, a drain upon the Will's resources. We are very limited in our abilities. Because Roum has a surplus of Watchers, we all are on short rations as it is, and if we admit you our rations will be all the shorter."

"But where will I go? What shall I do?"

"I advise you," he said blandly, "to throw yourself upon the mercy of the Prince of Roum."

3

Outside, I told that to Gormon, and he doubled with laughter, guffawing so furiously that the striations on his lean cheeks blazed like bloody stripes. "The mercy of the Prince of Roum!" he repeated. "The mercy—of the Prince of Roum—"

"It is customary for the unfortunate to seek the aid of the local ruler," I said coldly.

"The Prince of Roum knows no mercy," Gormon told me. "The Prince of Roum will feed you your own limbs to ease your hunger!"

"Perhaps," Avluela put in, "we should try to find the Fliers' Lodge. They'll feed us there."

"Not Gormon," I observed. "We have obligations to one another."

"We could bring food out to him," she said.

"I prefer to visit the court first," I insisted. "Let us make sure of our status. Afterward we can improvise living arrangements, if we must."

She yielded, and we made our way to the palace of the Prince of Roum, a massive building fronted by a colossal column-ringed plaza, on the far side of the river that splits the city. In the plaza we were accosted by mendicants of many sorts, some not even Earthborn; something with ropy tendrils and a corrugated, noseless face thrust itself at me and jabbered for alms until Gormon pushed it away, and moments later a second creature, equally strange, its skin pocked with luminescent craters and its limbs studded with eyes, embraced my knees and pleaded in the name of the Will for my mercy. "I am only a poor Watcher," I said, indicating my cart, "and am here to gain mercy myself." But the being persisted, sobbing out its misfortunes in a blurred, feathery voice, and in the end, to Gormon's immense disgust, I dropped a few food tablets into the shelf-like pouch on its chest. Then we muscled on toward the doors of the palace. At the portico a more horrid sight presented itself: a maimed Flier, fragile limbs bent and twisted, one wing half-unfolded and severely cropped, the other missing altogether. The Flier rushed upon Avluela, called her by a name not hers, moistened her leggings with tears so copious that

the fur of them matted and stained. "Sponsor me to the lodge," he appealed. "They have turned me away because I am crippled, but if you sponsor me—" Avluela explained that she could do nothing, that she was a stranger to this lodge. The broken Flier would not release her, and Gormon with great delicacy lifted him like the bundle of dry bones that he was and set him aside. We stepped up onto the portico and at once were confronted by a trio of soft-faced neuters, who asked our business and admitted us quickly to the next line of barrier, which was manned by a pair of wizened Indexers. Speaking in unison, they queried us.

"We seek audience," I said. "A matter of mercy."

"The day of audience is four days hence," said the Indexer on the right. "We will enter your request on the rolls."

"We have no place to sleep!" Avluela burst out. "We are hungry! We—"

I hushed her. Gormon, meanwhile, was groping in the mouth of his overpocket. Bright things glimmered in his hand: pieces of gold, the eternal metal, stamped with hawk-nosed, bearded faces. He had found them grubbing in the ruins. He tossed one coin to the Indexer who had refused us. The man snapped it from the air, rubbed his thumb roughly across its shining obverse, and dropped it instantly into a fold of his garment. The second Indexer waited expectantly. Smiling, Gormon gave him his coin.

"Perhaps," I said, "we can arrange for a special audience within."

"Perhaps you can," said one of the Indexers. "Go through."

And so we passed into the nave of the palace itself and stood in the great, echoing space, looking down the central aisle toward the shielded throne-chamber at the apse. There were more beggars in here—licensed ones holding hereditary concessions—and also throngs of Pilgrims, Communicants, Rememberers, Musicians, Scribes, and Indexers. I heard muttered prayers; I smelled the scent of spicy incense; I felt the vibration of subterranean gongs. In cycles past, this building had been a shrine of one of the old religions—the Christers, Gormon told me, making me suspect once more that he was a Rememberer masquerading as a Changeling—and it still maintained something of its holy character even though it served as Roum's seat of secular government. But how were we to get to see the Prince? To my left I saw a small ornate chapel which a line of prosperous-looking Merchants and Landholders was slowly entering. Peering past them, I noted three skulls mounted on an interrogation fixture—a memory-tank input—and beside them, a burly Scribe. Telling Gormon and Avluela to wait for me in the aisle, I joined the line.

It moved infrequently, and nearly an hour passed before I reached the interrogation fixture. The skulls glared sightlessly at me; within their sealed crania, nutrient fluids

bubbled and gurgled, caring for the dead, yet still functional, brains whose billion billion synaptic units now served as incomparable mnemonic devices. The Scribe seemed aghast to find a Watcher in this line, but before he could challenge me I blurted, "I come as a stranger to claim the Prince's mercy. I and my companions are without lodging. My own guild has turned me away. What shall I do? How may I gain an audience?"

"Come back in four days."

"I've slept on the road for more days than that. Now I must rest more easily."

"A public inn—"

"But I am guilded!" I protested. "The public inns would not admit me while my guild maintains an inn here, and my guild refuses me because of some new regulation, and—you see my predicament?"

In a wearied voice the Scribe said, "You may have application for a special audience. It will be denied, but you may apply."

"Where?"

"Here. State your purpose."

I identified myself to the skulls by my public designation, listed the names and status of my two companions, and explained my case. All this was absorbed and transmitted to the ranks of brains mounted somewhere in the depths of the city, and when I was done the Scribe said, "If the application is approved, you will be notified."

"Meanwhile where shall I stay?"

"Close to the palace, I would suggest."

I understood. I could join that legion of un-

fortunates packing the plaza. How many of them had requested some special favor of the Prince and were still there, months or years later, waiting to be summoned to the Presence? Sleeping on stone, begging for crusts, living in foolish hope!

But I had exhausted my avenues. I returned to Gormon and Avluela, told them of the situation, and suggested that we now attempt to hunt whatever accommodations we could. Gormon, guildless, was welcome at any of the squalid public inns maintained for his kind; Avluela could probably find residence at her own guild's lodge; only I would have to sleep in the streets—and not for the first time. But I hoped that we would not have to separate. I had come to think of us as a family, strange thought though that was for a Watcher.

As we moved toward the exit, my timepiece told me softly that the hour of Watching had come round again. It was my obligation and my privilege to tend to my Watching wherever I might be, regardless of the circumstances, whenever my hour came round; and so I halted, opened the cart, activated the equipment. Gormon and Avluela stood beside me. I saw smirks and open mockery on the faces of those who passed in and out of the palace; Watching was not held in very high repute, for we had Watched so long, and the promised enemy had never come. Yet one has one's duties, comic though they may seem to others. What is a hollow ritual to some is a life's work to others. Doggedly I forced my-

self into a state of Watchfulness. The world melted away from me, and I plunged into the heavens. The familiar joy engulfed me; and I searched the familiar places, and some that were not so familiar, my amplified mind leaping through the galaxies in wild swoops. Was an armada massing? Were troops drilling for the conquest of Earth? Four times a day I Watched, and the other members of my guild did the same, each at slightly different hours, so that no moment went by without some vigilant mind on guard. I do not believe that that was a foolish calling.

When I came up from my trance, a brazen voice was crying, "—for the Prince of Roum! Make way for the Prince of Roum!"

I blinked and caught my breath and fought to shake off the last strands of my concentration. A gilded palanquin borne by a phalanx of neuters had emerged from the rear of the palace and was proceeding down the nave toward me. Four men in the elegant costumes and brilliant masks of the guild of Masters flanked the litter, and it was preceded by a trio of Changelings, squat and broad, whose throats were so modified to imitate the sounding-boxes of bullfrogs; they emitted a trumpetlike boom of majestic sound as they advanced. It struck me as most strange that a prince would admit Changelings to his service, even ones as gifted as these.

My cart was blocking the progress of this magnificent procession, and hastily I struggled to close it and move it aside before the parade swept down upon me. Age and fear

made my fingers tremble, and I could not make the sealings properly; while I fumbled in increasing clumsiness, the strutting Changelings drew so close that the blare of their throats was deafening, and Gormon attempted to aid me, forcing me to hiss at him that it is forbidden for anyone not of my guild to touch the equipment. I pushed him away; and an instant later a vanguard of neuters descended on me and prepared to scourge me from the spot with sparkling whips. "In the Will's name," I cried, "I am a Watcher!"

And in antiphonal response came the deep, calm, enormous reply, "Let him be. He is a Watcher."

All motion ceased. The Prince of Roum had spoken.

The neuters drew back. The Changelings halted their music. The bearers of the palanquin eased it to the floor. All those in the nave of the palace had pulled back, save only Gormon and Avluela and myself. The shimmering chain-curtains of the palanquin parted. Two of the Masters hurried forward and thrust their hands through the sonic barrier within, offering aid to their monarch. The barrier died away with a whimpering buzz.

The Prince of Roum appeared.

He was so young! He was nothing more than a boy, his hair full and dark, his face unlined. But he had been born to rule, and for all his youth he was as commanding as anyone I had ever seen. His lips were thin and tightly compressed; his aquiline nose was sharp and aggressive; his eyes, deep and cold,

were infinite pools. He wore the jeweled garments of the guild of Dominators, but incised on his cheek was the double-barred cross of the Defenders, and around his neck he carried the dark shawl of the Rememberers. A Dominator may enroll in as many guilds as he pleases, and it would be a strange thing for a Dominator not also to be a Defender; but it startled me to find this prince a Rememberer as well. That is not normally a guild for the fierce.

He looked at me with little interest and said, "You choose an odd place to do your Watching, old man."

"The hour chose the place, sire," I replied. "I was here, and my duty compelled me. I had no way of knowing that you were about to come forth."

"Your Watching found no enemies?"

"None, sire."

I was about to press my luck, to take advantage of the unexpected appearance of the Prince to beg for his aid; but his interest in me died like a guttering candle as I stood there, and I did not dare call to him when his head had turned. He eyed Gormon a long moment, frowning and tugging at his chin. Then his gaze fell on Avluela. His eyes brightened. His jaw muscles flickered. His delicate nostrils widened. "Come up here, little Flier," he said, beckoning. "Are you this Watcher's friend?"

She nodded, terrified.

The Prince held out a hand to her and grasped; she floated up onto the palanquin,

and with a grin so evil it seemed a parody of wickedness, the young Dominator drew her through the curtain. Instantly a pair of Masters restored the sonic barrier, but the procession did not move on. I stood mute. Gormon beside me was frozen, his powerful body rigid as a rod. I wheeled my cart to a less conspicuous place. Long moments passed. The courtiers remained silent, discreetly looking away from the palanquin.

At length the curtain parted once more. Avluela came stumbling out, her face pale, her eyes blinking rapidly. She seemed dazed. Streaks of sweat gleamed on her cheeks. She nearly fell, and a neuter caught her and swung her down to floor level. Beneath her jacket her wings were partly erect, giving her a hunchbacked look and telling me that she was in great emotional distress. In ragged, sliding steps she came to us, quivering, wordless; she darted a glance at me and flung herself against Gormon's broad chest.

The bearers lifted the palanquin. The Prince of Roum went out from his palace.

When he was gone, Avluela stammered hoarsely, "The Prince has granted us lodging in the royal hostelry!"

4

The hostelkeepers, of course, would not believe us.

Guests of the Prince were housed in the royal hostelry, which was to the rear of the palace in a small garden of frostflowers and blossoming ferns. The usual inhabitants of such a hostelry were Masters and an occasional Dominator; sometimes a particularly important Rememberer on an errand of research would win a niche there, or some highly placed Defender visiting for purposes of strategic planning. To house a Flier in a royal hostelry was distinctly odd; to admit a Watcher was unlikely; to take in a Changeling or some other guildless person was improbable beyond comprehension. When we presented ourselves, therefore, we were met by Servitors whose attitude was at first one of high good humor at our joke, then of irritation, finally of scorn. "Get away," they told us ultimately. "Scum! Rabble!"

Avluela said in a grave voice, "The Prince has granted us lodging here, and you may not refuse us."

"Away! Away!"

One snaggle-toothed Servitor produced a neural truncheon and brandished it in Gormon's face, passing a foul remark about his guildlessness. Gormon slapped the truncheon from the man's grasp, oblivious to the painful sting, and kicked him in the gut, so that he coiled and fell over, puking. Instantly

a throng of neuters came rushing from within the hostelry. Gormon seized another of the Servitors and hurled him into the midst of them, turning them into a muddled mob. Wild shouts and angry cursing cries attracted the attention of a venerable Scribe who waddled to the door, bellowed for silence, and interrogated us. "That's easily checked," he said, when Avluela had told the story. To a Servitor he said contemptuously, "Send a think to the Indexers, fast!"

In time the confusion was untangled and we were admitted. We were given separate but adjoining rooms. I had never known such luxury before, and perhaps never shall again. The rooms were long, high, and deep. One entered them through telescopic pits keyed to one's own thermal output, to assure privacy. Lights glowed at the resident's merest nod, for hanging from ceiling globes and nestling in cupolas on the walls were spicules of slavelight from one of the Brightstar worlds, trained through suffering to obey such commands. The windows came and went at the dweller's whim; when not in use, they were concealed by streamers of quasi-sentient outworld gauzes, which not only were decorative in their own right, but which functioned as monitors to produce delightful scents according to requisitioned patterns. The rooms were equipped with individual thinking caps connected to the main memory banks. They likewise had conduits that summoned Servitors, Scribes, Indexers, or Musicians as required. Of course, a man of my own humble

guild would not deign to make use of other human beings that way, out of fear of their glowering resentment; but in any case I had little need of them.

I did not ask of Avluela what had occurred in the Prince's palanquin to bring us such bounty. I could well imagine, as could Gormon, whose barely suppressed inner rage was eloquent of his never-admitted love for my pale, slender little Flier.

We settled in. I placed my cart beside the window, draped it with gauzes, and left it in readiness for my next period of Watching. I cleaned my body of grime while entities mounted in the wall sang me to peace. Later I ate. Afterwards Avluela came to me, refreshed and relaxed, and sat beside me in my room as we talked of our experiences. Gormon did not appear for hours. I thought that perhaps he had left this hostelry altogether, finding the atmosphere too rarefied for him, and had sought company among his own guildless kind. But at twilight, Avluela and I walked in the cloistered courtyard of the hostelry and mounted a ramp to watch the stars emerge in Roum's sky, and Gormon was there. With him was a lanky and emaciated man in a Rememberer's shawl; they were talking in low tones.

Gormon nodded to me and said, "Watcher, meet my new friend."

The emaciated one fingered his shawl. "I am the Rememberer Basil," he intoned, in a voice as thin as a fresco that has been peeled from its wall. "I have come from Perris to

delve into the mysteries of Roum. I shall be here many years."

"The Rememberer has fine stories to tell," said Gormon. "He is among the foremost of his guild. As you approached, he was describing to me the techniques by which the past is revealed. They drive a trench through the strata of Third Cycle deposits, you see, and with vacuum cores they lift the molecules of earth to lay bare the ancient layers."

"We have found," Basil said, "the catacombs of Imperial Roum, and the rubble of the Time of Sweeping, the books inscribed on slivers of white metal, written toward the close of the Second Cycle. All these go to Perris for examination and classification and decipherment; then they return. Does the past interest you, Watcher?"

"To some extent." I smiled. "This Changeling here shows much more fascination for it. I sometimes suspect his authenticity. Would you recognize a Rememberer in disguise?"

Basil scrutinized Gormon; he lingered over the bizarre features, the excessively muscular frame. "He is no Rememberer," he said at length. "But I agree that he has antiquarian interests. He has asked me many profound questions."

"Such as?"

"He wishes to know the origin of guilds. He asks the name of the genetic surgeon who crafted the first true-breeding Fliers. He wonders why there are Changelings, and if they are truly under the curse of the Will."

"And do you have answers for these?" I asked.

"For some," said Basil. "For some."

"The origin of guilds?"

"To give structure and meaning to a society that has suffered defeat and destruction," said the Rememberer. "At the end of the Second Cycle all was in flux. No man knew his rank nor his purpose. Through our world strode haughty outworlders who looked upon us all as worthless. It was necessary to establish fixed frames of reference by which one man might know his value beside another. So the first guilds appeared: Dominators, Masters, Merchants, Landholders, Vendors and Servitors. Then came Scribes, Musicians, Clowns and Transporters. Afterward Indexers became necessary, and then Watchers and Defenders. When the Years of Magic gave us Fliers and Changelings, those guilds were added, and then the guildless ones, the neuters, were produced, so that—"

"But surely the Changelings are guildless too!" said Avluela.

The Rememberer looked at her for the first time. "Who are you, child?"

"Avluela of the Fliers. I travel with this Watcher and this Changeling."

Basil said, "As I have been telling the Changeling here, in the early days his kind was guilded. The guild was dissolved a thousand years ago by the order of the Council of Dominators after an attempt by a disreputable Changeling faction to seize control of the holy places of Jorslem, and since that time

Changelings have been guildless, ranking only above neuters."

"I never knew that," I said.

"You are no Rememberer," said Basil smugly. "It is our craft to uncover the past."

"True. True."

Gormon said, "And today, how many guilds are there?"

Discomfited, Basil replied vaguely, "At least a hundred, my friend. Some are quite small; some are local. I am concerned only with the original guilds and their immediate successors; what has happened in the past few hundred years is in the province of others. Shall I requisition an information for you?"

"Never mind," Gormon said. "It was only an idle question."

"Your curiosity is well developed," said the Rememberer.

"I find the world and all it contains extremely fascinating. Is this sinful?"

"It is strange," said Basil. "The guildless rarely look beyond their own horizons."

A Servitor appeared. With a mixture of awe and contempt he genuflected before Avluela and said, "The Prince has returned. He desires your company in the palace at this time."

Terror glimmered in Avluela's eyes. But to refuse was inconceivable. "Shall I come with you?" she asked.

"Please. You must be robed and perfumed. He wishes you to come to him with your wings open, as well."

Avluela nodded. The Servitor led her away.

We remained on the ramp a while longer; the Rememberer Basil talked of the old days of Roum, and I listened, and Gormon peered into the gathering darkness. Eventually, his throat dry, the Rememberer excused himself and moved solemnly away. A few moments later, in the courtyard below us, a door opened and Avluela emerged, walking as though she were of the guild of Somnambulists, not of Fliers. She was nude under transparent draperies, and her fragile body gleamed ghostly white in the starbeams. Her wings were spread and fluttered slowly in a somber systole and diastole. One Servitor grasped each of her elbows: they seemed to be propelling her toward the palace as though she were but a dreamed facsimile of herself and not a real woman.

"Fly, Avluela, fly," Gormon growled. "Escape while you can!"

She disappeared into a side entrance of the palace.

The Changeling looked at me. "She has sold herself to the Prince to provide lodging for us."

"So it seems."

"I could smash down that palace!"

"You love her?"

"It should be obvious."

"Cure yourself," I advised. "You are an unusual man, but still a Flier is not for you. Particularly a Flier who has shared the bed of the Prince of Roum."

"She goes from my arms to his."

I was staggered. "You've known her?"

"More than once," he said, smiling sadly. "At the moment of ecstasy her wings thrash like leaves in a storm."

I gripped the railing of the ramp so that I would not tumble into the courtyard. The stars whirled overhead; the old moon and its two blank-faced consorts leaped and bobbed. I was shaken without fully understanding the cause of my emotion. Was it wrath that Gormon had dared to violate a canon of the law? Was it a manifestation of those pseudo-parental feelings I had toward Avluela? Or was it mere envy of Gormon for daring to commit a sin beyond my capacity, though not beyond my desires?

I said, "They could burn your brain for that. They could mince your soul. And now you make me an accessory."

"What of it? That Prince commands, and he gets—but others have been there before him. I had to tell someone."

"Enough. Enough."

"Will we see her again?"

"Princes tire quickly of their women. A few days, perhaps a single night—then he will throw her back to us. And perhaps then we shall have to leave this hostelry." I sighed. "At least we'll have known it a few nights more than we deserved."

"Where will you go then?" Gormon asked.

"I will stay in Roum awhile."

"Even if you sleep in the streets? There does not seem to be much demand for Watchers here."

"I'll manage," I said. "Then I may go toward Perris."

"To learn from the Rememberers?"

"To see Perris. What of you? What do you want in Roum?"

"Avluela."

"Stop that talk!"

"Very well," he said, and his smile was bitter. "But I will stay here until the Prince is through with her. Then she will be mine, and we'll find ways to survive. The guildless are resourceful. They have to be. Maybe we'll scrounge lodgings in Roum awhile, and then follow you to Perris. If you're willing to travel with monsters and faithless Fliers."

I shrugged. "We'll see about that when the time comes."

"Have you ever been in the company of a Changeling before?"

"Not often. Not for long."

"I'm honored." He drummed on the parapet. "Don't cast me off, Watcher. I have a reason for wanting to stay with you."

"Which is?"

"To see your face on the day your machines tell you that the invasion of Earth has begun."

I let myself sag forward, shoulders drooping. "You'll stay with me a long time, then."

"Don't you believe the invasion is coming?"

"Some day. Not soon."

Gormon chuckled. "You're wrong. It's almost here."

"You don't amuse me."

"What is it, Watcher? Have you lost your faith? It's been known for a thousand years: another race covets Earth and owns it by treaty, and will some day come to collect. That much was decided at the end of the Second Cycle."

"I know all that, and I am no Rememberer." Then I turned to him and spoke words I never thought I would say aloud. "For twice your lifetime, Changeling, I've listened to the stars and done my Watching. Something done that often loses meaning. Say your own name ten thousand times and it will be an empty sound. I have Watched, and Watched well, and in the dark hours of the night I sometimes think I Watch for nothing, that I have wasted my life. There is a pleasure in Watching, but perhaps there is no real purpose."

His hand encircled my wrist. "Your confession is as shocking as mine. Keep your faith, Watcher. The invasion comes!"

"How could you possibly know?"

"The guildless also have their skills."

The conversation troubled me. I said, "Is it painful to be guildless?"

"One grows reconciled. And there are certain freedoms to compensate for the lack of status. I may speak freely to all."

"I notice."

"I move freely. I am always sure of food and lodging, though the food may be rotten and the lodging poor. Women are attracted to me despite all prohibitions. Because of them, perhaps. I am untroubled by ambitions."

"Never desire to rise above your rank?"

"Never."

"You might have been happier as a Rememberer."

"I am happy now. I can have a Rememberer's pleasures without his responsibility."

"How smug you are!" I cried. "To make a virtue of guildlessness!"

"How else does one endure the weight of the Will?" He looked toward the palace. "The humble rise. The mighty fall. Take this as prophecy, Watcher: that lusty Prince in there will know more of life before summer comes. I'll rip out his eyes for taking Avluela!"

"Strong words. You bubble with treason tonight."

"Take it as prophecy."

"You can't get close to him," I said. Then, irritated for taking his foolishness seriously, I added, "And why blame him? He only does as princes do. Blame the girl for going to him. She might have refused."

"And lost her wings. Or died. No, she had no choice. I do!" In a sudden, terrible gesture the Changeling held out thumb and forefinger, double-jointed, long-nailed, and plunged them forward into imagined eyes. "Wait," he said. "You'll see!"

In the courtyard two Chronomancers appeared, set up the apparatus of their guild, and lit tapers by which to read the shape of tomorrow. A sickly odor of pallid smoke rose to my nostrils. I had now lost further desire to speak with the Changeling.

"It grows late," I said. "I need rest, and soon I must do my Watching."

"Watch carefully," Gormon told me.

5

At night in my chamber I performed my fourth and last Watch of that long day, and for the first time in my life I detected an anomaly. I could not interpret it. It was an obscure sensation, a mingling of tastes and sounds, a feeling of being in contact with some colossal mass. Worried, I clung to my instruments far longer than usual, but perceived no more clearly at the end of my seance than at its commencement.

Afterward I wondered about my obligations.

Watchers are trained from childhood to be swift to sound the alarm; and the alarm must be sounded when the Watcher judges the world in peril. Was I now obliged to notify the Defenders? Four times in my life the alarm had been given, on each occasion in error; and each Watcher who had thus touched off a false mobilization had suffered a fearful loss of status. One had contributed his brain to the memory tanks; one had be-

come a neuter out of shame; one had smashed his instruments and gone to live among the guildless; and one, vainly attempting to continue in his profession, had discovered himself mocked by all his comrades. I saw no virtue in scorning one who had delivered a false alarm, for was it not preferable for a Watcher to cry out too soon than not at all? But those were the customs of our guild, and I was constrained by them.

I evaluated my position and decided that I did not have valid grounds for an alarm.

I reflected that Gormon had placed suggestive ideas in my mind that evening. I might possibly be reacting only to his jeering talk of imminent invasion.

I could not act. I dared not jeopardize my standing by hasty outcry. I mistrusted my own emotional state.

I gave no alarm.

Seething, confused, my soul roiling, I closed my cart and let myself sink into a drugged sleep.

At dawn I woke and rushed to the window, expecting to find invaders in the streets. But all was still; a winter grayness hung over the courtyard, and sleepy Servitors pushed passive neuters about. Uneasily I did my first Watching of the day, and to my relief the strangenesses of the night before did not return, although I had it in mind that my sensitivity is always greater at night than upon arising.

I ate and went to the courtyard. Gormon and Avluela were already there. She looked

fatigued and downcast, depleted by her night with the Prince of Roum, but I said nothing to her about it. Gormon, slouching disdainfully against a wall embellished with the shells of radiant mollusks, said to me, "Did your Watching go well?"

"Well enough."

"What of the day?"

"Out to roam Roum," I said. "Will you come? Avluela? Gormon?"

"Surely," he said, and she gave a faint nod; and, like the tourists we were, we set off to inspect the splendid city of Roum.

Gormon acted as our guide to the jumbled pasts of Roum, belying his claim never to have been here before. As well as any Rememberer he described the things we saw as wc walked the winding streets. All the scattered levels of thousands of years were exposed. We saw the power domes of the Second Cycle, and the Colosseum where at an unimaginably early date man and beast contended like jungle creatures. In the broken hull of that building of horrors Gormon told us of the savagery of that unimaginably ancient time. "They fought," he said, "naked before huge throngs. With bare hands men challenged beasts called lions, great hairy cats with swollen heads; and when the lion lay in its gore, the victor turned to the Prince of Roum and asked to be pardoned for whatever crime it was that had cast him into the arena. And if he had fought well, the Prince made a gesture with his hand, and the man was freed." Gormon made the gesture for us:

a thumb upraised and jerked backward over the right shoulder several times. "But if the man had shown cowardice, or if the lion had distinguished itself in the manner of its dying, the Prince made another gesture, and the man was condemned to be slain by a second beast." Gormon showed us that gesture too: the middle finger jutting upward from a clenched fist and lifted in a short sharp thrust.

"How are these things known?" Avluela asked, but Gormon pretended not to hear her.

We saw the line of fusion-pylons built early in the Third Cycle to draw energy from the world's core; they were still functioning, although stained and corroded. We saw the shattered stump of a Second Cycle weather machine, still a mighty column at least twenty men high. We saw a hill on which white marble relics of First Cycle Roum sprouted like pale clumps of winter deathflowers. Penetrating toward the inner part of the city, we came upon the embankment of defensive amplifiers waiting in readiness to hurl the full impact of the Will against invaders. We viewed a market where visitors from the stars haggled with peasants for excavated fragments of antiquity. Gormon strode into the crowd and made several purchases. We came to a fleshhouse for travelers from afar, where one could buy anything from quasi-life to mounds of passion-ice. We ate at a small restaurant by the edge of the River Tver, where guildless ones were served without ceremony, and at Gormon's insistence we

dined on mounds of a soft doughy substance and drank a tart yellow wine, local specialties.

Afterward we passed through a covered arcade in whose many aisles plump Vendors peddled star-goods, costly trinkets from Afreek, and the flimsy constructs of the local Manufactories. Just beyond we emerged in a plaza that contained a fountain in the shape of a boat, and to the rear of this rose a flight of cracked and battered stone-stairs ascending to a zone of rubble and weeds. Gormon beckoned, and we scrambled into this dismal area, then passed rapidly through it to a place where a sumptuous palace, by its looks early Second Cycle or even First, brooded over a sloping vegetated hill.

"They say this is the center of the world," Gormon declared. "In Jorslem one finds another place that also claims the honor. They mark the spot here by a map."

How can the world have one center," Avluela asked, "when it is round?"

Gormon laughed. We went in. Within, in wintry darkness, there stood a colossal jeweled globe lit by some inner glow.

"Here is your world," said Gormon, gesturing grandly.

"Oh!" Avluela gasped. "Everything! Everything is here!"

The map was a masterpiece of craftsmanship. It showed natural contours and elevations, its seas seemed deep liquid pools, its deserts were so parched as to make thirst spring in one's mouth, its cities swirled with

vigor and life. I beheld the continents, Eyrop, Afreek, Ais, Stralya. I saw the vastness of Earth Ocean. I traversed the golden span of Land Bridge, which I had crossed so toilfully on foot not long before. Avluela rushed forward and pointed to Roum, to Agupt, to Jorslem, to Perris. She tapped the globe at the high mountains north of Hind and said softly, "This is where I was born, where the ice lives, where the mountains touch the moons. Here is where the Fliers have their kingdom." She ran a finger westward toward Fars and beyond it into the terrible Arban Desert, and on to Agupt. "This is where I flew. By night, when I left my girlhood. We all must fly, and I flew here. A hundred times I thought I would die. Here, here in the desert, sand in my throat as I flew, sand beating against my wings—I was forced down, I lay naked on the hot sand for days, and another Flier saw me, he came down to me and pitied me, and lifted me up, and when I was aloft my strength returned, and we flew on toward Agupt. And he died over the sea, his life stopped though he was young and strong, and he fell down into the sea, and I flew down to be with him, and the water was hot even at night. I drifted, and morning came, and I saw the living stones growing like trees in the water, and the fish of many colors, and they came to him and pecked at his flesh as he floated with his wings outspread on the water, and I left him, I thrust him down to rest there, and I rose, and I flew on to Agupt, alone, frightened, and there I met you, Watcher." Timidly she

smiled to me. "Show us the place where you were young, Watcher."

Painfully, for I was suddenly stiff at the knees, I hobbled to the far side of the globe. Avluela followed me; Gormon hung back, as though not interested at all. I pointed to the scattered islands rising in two long strips from Earth Ocean—the remnants of the Lost Continents.

"Here," I said, indicating my native island in the west. "I was born here."

"So far away!" Avluela cried.

"And so long ago," I said. "In the middle of the Second Cycle, it sometimes seems to me."

"No! That is not possible!" But she looked at me as though it might just be true that I was thousands of years old.

I smiled and touched her satiny cheek. "It only seems that way to me," I said.

"When did you leave your home?"

"When I was twice your age," I said. "I came first to here—" I indicated the eastern group of islands. "I spent a dozen years as a Watcher on Palash. Then the Will moved me to cross Earth Ocean to Afreek. I came. I lived awhile in the hot countries. I went on to Agupt. I met a certain small Flier." Falling silent, I looked a long while at the islands that had been my home, and within my mind my image changed from the gaunt and eroded thing I now had become, and I saw myself young and well-fleshed, climbing the green mountains and swimming in the chill sea, doing my Watching at the rim of a white beach hammered by surf.

While I brooded Avluela turned away from me to Gormon and said, "Now you. Show us where you came from, Changeling!"

Gormon shrugged. "The place does not appear to be on this globe."

"But that's *impossible*!"

"Is it?" he asked.

She pressed him, but he evaded her, and we passed through a side exit and into the streets of Roum.

I was growing tired, but Avluela hungered for this city and wished to devour it all in an afternoon, and so we went on through a maze of interlocking streets, through a zone of sparkling mansions of Masters and Merchants, and through a foul den of Servitors and Vendors that extended into subterranean catacombs, and to a place where Clowns and Musicians resorted, and to another where the guild of Somnambulists offered its doubtful wares. A bloated female Somnambulist begged us to come inside and buy the truth that comes with trances, and Avluela urged us to go, but Gormon shook his head and I smiled, and we moved on. Now we were at the edge of a park close to the city's core. Here the citizens of Roum promenaded with an energy rarely seen in hot Agupt, and we joined the parade.

"Look there!" Avluela said. "How bright it is!"

She pointed toward the shining arc of a dimensional sphere enclosing some relic of the ancient city; shading my eyes, I could make out a weathered stone wall within, and a knot

of people. Gormon said, "It is the Mouth of Truth."

"What is that?" Avluela asked.

"Come. See."

A line progressed into the sphere. We joined it and soon were at the lip of the interior, peering at the timeless region just across the threshold. Why this relic and so few others had been accorded such special protection I did not know, and I asked Gormon, whose knowledge was so unaccountably as profound as any Rememberer's, and he replied, "Because this is the realm of certainty, where what one says is absolutely congruent with what actually is the case."

"I don't understand," said Avluela.

"It is impossible to lie in this place," Gormon told her. "Can you imagine any relic more worthy of protection?" He stepped across the entry duct, blurring as he did so, and I followed him quickly within. Avluela hesitated. It was a long moment before she entered; pausing a moment on the very threshold, she seemed buffeted by the wind that blew along the line of demarcation between the outer world and the pocket universe in which we stood.

An inner compartment held the Mouth of Truth itself. The line extended toward it, and a solemn Indexer was controlling the flow of entry to the tabernacle. It was a while before we three were permitted to go in. We found ourselves before the ferocious head of a monster in high relief, affixed to an ancient wall pockmarked by time. The monster's jaws

gaped; the open mouth was a dark and sinister hole. Gormon nodded, inspecting it, as though he seemed pleased to find it exactly as he had thought it would be.

"What do we do?" Avluela asked.

Gormon said, "Watcher, put your right hand into the Mouth of Truth."

Frowning, I complied.

"Now," said Gormon, "one of us asks a question. You must answer it. If you speak anything but the truth, the mouth will close and sever your hand."

"No!" Avluela cried.

I stared uneasily at the stone jaws rimming my wrist. A Watcher without both his hands is a man without a craft; in Second Cycle days one might have obtained a prosthesis more artful than one's original hand, but the Second Cycle had long ago been concluded, and such niceties were not to be purchased on Earth nowadays.

"How is such a thing possible?" I asked.

"The Will is unusually strong in these precincts," Gormon replied. "It distinguishes sternly between truth and untruth. To the rear of this wall sleeps a trio of Somnambulists through whom the Will speaks, and they control the Mouth. Do you fear the Will, Watcher?"

"I fear my own tongue."

"Be brave. Never has a lie been told before this wall. Never has a hand been lost."

"Go ahead, then," I said. "Who will ask me a question?"

"I," said Gormon. "Tell me, Watcher: all

pretense aside, would you say that a life spent in Watching has been a life spent wisely?"

I was silent a long moment, rotating my thoughts, eyeing the jaws.

At length I said, "To devote oneself to vigilance on behalf of one's fellow man is perhaps the noblest purpose one can serve."

"Careful!" Gormon cried in alarm.

"I am not finished," I said.

"Go on."

"But to devote oneself to vigilance when the enemy is an imaginary one is idle, and to congratulate oneself for looking long and well for a foe that is not coming is foolish and sinful. My life has been a waste."

The jaws of the Mouth of Truth did not quiver.

I removed my hand. I stared at it as though it had newly sprouted from my wrist. I felt suddenly several cycles old. Avluela, her eyes wide, her hands to her lips, seemed shocked by what I had said. My own words appeared to hang congealed in the air before the hideous idol.

"Spoken honestly," said Gormon, "although without much mercy for yourself. You judge yourself too harshly, Watcher."

"I spoke to save my hand," I said. "Would you have had me lie?"

He smiled. To Avluela the Changeling said, "Now it's your turn."

Visibly frightened, the little Flier approached the Mouth. Her dainty hand trembled as she inserted it between the slabs of cold stone. I fought back an urge to rush to-

ward her and pull her free of that devilish grimacing head.

"Who will question her?" I asked.

"I," said Gormon.

Avluela's wings stirred faintly beneath her garments. Her face grew pale; her nostrils flickered; her upper lip slid over the lower one. She stood slouched against the wall and stared in horror at the termination of her arm. Outside the chamber vague faces peered at us; lips moved in what no doubt were expressions of impatience over our lengthy visit to the Mouth; but we heard nothing. The atmosphere around us was warm and clammy, with a musty tang like that which would come from a well that was driven through the structure of Time.

Gormon said slowly, "This night past you allowed your body to be possessed by the Prince of Roum. Before that, you granted yourself to the Changeling Gormon, although such liaisons are forbidden by custom and law. Much prior to that you were the mate of a Flier, now deceased. You may have had other men, but I know nothing of them, and for the purposes of my question they are not relevant. Tell me this, Avluela: which of the three gave you the most intense physical pleasure, which of the three aroused your deepest emotions, and which of the three would you choose as a mate, if you were choosing a mate?"

I wanted to protest that the Changeling had asked her three questions, not one, and so had taken unfair advantage. But I had no

chance to speak, because Avluela replied unfalteringly, hand wedged deep into the Mouth of Truth, "The Prince of Roum gave me greater pleasure of the body than I had ever known before, but he is cold and cruel, and I despise him. My dead Flier I loved more deeply than any person before or since, but he was weak, and I would not have wanted a weakling as a mate. You, Gormon, seem almost a stranger to me even now, and I feel that I know neither your body nor your soul, and yet, though the gulf between us is so wide, it is you with whom I would spend my days to come."

She drew her hand from the Mouth of Truth.

"Well spoken!" said Gormon, though the accuracy of her words had clearly wounded as well as pleased him. "Suddenly you find eloquence, eh, when the circumstances demand it. And now the turn is mine to risk my hand."

He neared the Mouth. I said, "You have asked the first two questions. Do you wish to finish the job and ask the third as well?"

"Hardly," he said. He made a negligent gesture with his free hand. "Put your heads together and agree on a joint question."

Avluela and I conferred. With uncharacteristic forwardness she proposed a question; and since it was the one I would have asked, I accepted it and told her to ask it.

She said, "When we stood before the globe of the world, Gormon, I asked you to show me the place where you were born, and you

said you were unable to find it on the map. That seemed most strange. Tell me now: are you what you say you are, a Changeling who wanders the world?"

He replied, "I am not."

In a sense he had satisfied the question as Avluela had phrased it; but it went without saying that his reply was inadequate, and he kept his hand in the Mouth of Truth as he continued, "I did not show my birthplace to you on the globe because I was born nowhere on this globe, but on a world of a star I must not name. I am no Changeling in your meaning of the word, though by some definitions I am, for my body is somewhat disguised, and on my own world I wear a different flesh. I have lived here ten years."

"What was your purpose in coming to Earth?" I asked.

"I am obliged only to answer one question," said Gormon. Then he smiled. "But I give you an answer anyway: I was sent to Earth in the capacity of a military observer, to prepare the way for the invasion for which you have Watched so long and in which you have ceased to believe, and which will be upon you in a matter now of some hours."

"Lies!" I bellowed. *"Lies!"*

Gormon laughed. And drew his hand from the Mouth of Truth, intact, unharmed.

6

Numb with confusion, I fled with my cart of instruments from that gleaming sphere and emerged into a street suddenly cold and dark. Night had come with winter's swiftness; it was almost the ninth hour, and almost the time for me to Watch once more.

Gormon's mockery thundered in my brain. He had arranged everything: he had maneuvered us in to the Mouth of Truth; he had wrung a confession of lost faith from me and a confession of a different sort from Avluela; he had mercilessly volunteered information he need not have revealed, spoken words calculated to split me to the core.

Was the Mouth of Truth a fraud? Could Gormon lie and emerge unscathed?

Never since I first took up my tasks had I Watched at anything but my appointed hours. This was a time of crumbling realities; I could not wait for the ninth hour to come round; crouching in the windy street, I opened my cart, readied my equipment, and sank like a diver into Watchfulness.

My amplified consciousness roared toward the stars.

Godlike I roamed infinity. I felt the rush of the solar wind, but I was no Flier to be hurled to destruction by that pressure, and I soared past it, beyond the reach of those angry particles of light, into the blackness at the edge of the sun's dominion. Down upon me there beat a different pressure.

Starships coming near.

Not the tourist lines bringing sightseers to gape at our diminished world. Not the registered mercantile transport vessels, nor the scoopships that collect the interstellar vapors, nor the resort craft on their hyperbolic orbits.

These were military craft, dark, alien, menacing. I could not tell their number; I knew only that they sped Earthward at many lights, nudging a cone of deflected energies before them; and it was that cone that I had sensed, that I had felt also the night before, booming into my mind through my instruments, engulfing me like a cube of crystal through which stress patterns play and shine.

All my life I had watched for this.

I had been trained to sense it. I had prayed that I never would sense it, and then in my emptiness I had prayed that I *would* sense it, and then I had ceased to believe in it. And then by grace of the Changeling Gormon, I had sensed it after all, Watching ahead of my hour, crouching in a cold Roumish street just outside the Mouth of Truth.

In his training, a Watcher is instructed to break from his Watchfulness as soon as his observations are confirmed by a careful check, so that he can sound the alarm. Obediently I made my check by shifting from one channel to another to another, triangulating and still picking up that foreboding sensation of titanic force rushing upon Earth at unimaginable speed.

Either I was deceived, or the invasion was

come. But I could not shake from my trance to give the alarm.

Lingeringly, lovingly, I drank in the sensory data for what seemed like hours. I fondled my equipment; I drained from it the total affirmation of faith that my readings gave me. Dimly I warned myself that I was wasting vital time, that it was my duty to leave this lewd caressing of destiny to summon the Defenders.

And at last I burst free of Watchfulness and returned to the world I was guarding.

Avluela was beside me; she was dazed, terrified, her knuckles to her teeth, her eyes blank.

"Watcher! Watcher, do you hear me? What's happening? What's going to happen?"

"The invasion," I said. "How long was I under?"

"About half a minute. I don't know. Your eyes were closed. I thought you were dead."

"Gormon was speaking the truth! The *invasion* is almost here. Where is he? Where did he go?"

"He vanished as we came away from that place with the Mouth," Avluela whispered. "Watcher, I'm frightened. I feel everything collapsing. I have to fly—I can't stay down here now!"

"Wait," I said, clutching at her and missing her arm. "Don't go now. First I have to give the alarm, and then—"

But she was already stripping off her clothing. Bare to the waist, her pale body gleamed in the evening light, while about us people

were rushing to and fro in ignorance of all that was about to occur. I wanted to keep Avluela beside me, but I could delay no longer in giving the alarm, and I turned away from her, back to my cart.

As though caught up in a dream born of overripe longings I reached for the node that I had never used, the one that would send forth a planetwide alert to the Defenders.

Had the alarm already been given? Had some other Watcher sensed what I had sensed, and, less paralyzed by bewilderment and doubt, performed a Watcher's final task?

No. No. For then I would be hearing the sirens' shriek reverberating from the orbiting loudspeakers above the city.

I touched the node. From the corner of my eye I saw Avluela, free of her encumbrances now, kneeling to say her words, filling her tender wings with strength. In a moment she would be in the air, beyond my grasp.

With a single swift tug I activated the alarm.

In that instant I became aware of a burly figure striding toward us. Gormon, I thought; and as I rose from my equipment I reached out to him; I wanted to seize him and hold him fast. But he who approached was not Gormon but some officious dough-faced Servitor who said to Avluela, "Go easy, Flier, let your wings drop. The Prince of Roum sends me to bring you to his presence."

He grappled with her. Her little breasts heaved; her eyes flashed anger at him.

"Let go of me! I'm going to fly!"

"The Prince of Roum summons you," the Servitor said, enclosing her in his heavy arms.

"The Prince of Roum will have other distractions tonight," I said. "He'll have no need of her."

As I spoke, the sirens began to sing from the skies.

The Servitor released her. His mouth worked noiselessly for an instant; he made one of the protective gestures of the Will; he looked skyward and grunted, "The alarm! Who gave the alarm? You, old Watcher?"

Figures rushed about insanely in the streets.

Avluela, freed, sped past me—on foot, her wings but half-furled—and was swallowed up in the surging throng. Over the terrifying sound of the sirens came booming messages from the public annunciators, giving instructions for defense and safety. A lanky man with the mark of the guild of Defenders upon his cheek rushed up to me, shouted words too incoherent to be understood, and sped on down the street. The world seemed to have gone mad.

Only I remained calm. I looked to the skies, half-expecting to see the invaders' black ships already hovering above the towers of Roum. But I saw nothing except the hovering night-lights and the other objects one might expect overhead.

"Gormon?" I called. "Avluela?"

I was alone.

A strange emptiness swept over me. I had

given the alarm; the invaders were on their way; I had lost my occupation. There was no need of Watchers now. Almost lovingly I touched the worn cart that had been my companion for so many years. I ran my fingers over its stained and pitted instruments; and then I looked away, abandoning it, and went down the dark streets cartless, burdenless, a man whose life had found and lost meaning in the same instant. And about me raged chaos.

7

It was understood that when the moment of Earth's final battle arrived, all guilds would be mobilized, the Watchers alone exempted. We who had manned the perimeter of defense for so long had no part in the strategy of combat; we were discharged by the giving of a true alarm. Now it was the time of the guild of Defenders to show its capabilities. They had planned for half a cycle what they would do in time of war. What plans would they call forth now? What deeds would they direct?

My only concern was to return to the royal hostelry and wait out the crisis. It was hope-

less to think of finding Avluela, and I pummeled myself savagely for having let her slip away, naked and without a protector, in that confused moment. Where would she go? Who would shield her?

A fellow Watcher, pulling his cart madly along, nearly collided with me. "Careful!" I snapped.

He looked up, breathless, stunned. "Is it true?" he asked. "The alarm?"

"Can't you hear?"

"But is it real?"

I pointed to his cart. "You know how to find that out."

"They say the man who gave the alarm was drunk, an old fool who was turned away from the inn yesterday."

"It could be so," I admitted.

"But if the alarm is real—!"

Smiling, I said, "If it is, now we all may rest. Good day to you, Watcher."

"Your cart! Where's your cart?" he shouted at me.

But I had moved past him, toward the mighty carven stone pillar of some relic of Imperial Roum.

Ancient images were carved on that pillar: battles and victories, foreign monarchs marched in the chains of disgrace through the streets of Roum, triumphant eagles celebrating imperial grandeur. In my strange new calmness I stood awhile before the column of stone and admired its elegant engravings. Toward me rushed a frenzied figure whom I recognized as the Rememberer Basil; I hailed

him, saying, "How timely you come! Do me the kindness of explaining these images, Rememberer. They fascinate me, and my curiosity is aroused."

"Are you insane? Can't you hear the alarm?"

"I gave the alarm, Rememberer."

"Flee, then! Invaders come! We must fight!"

"Not I, Basil. Now my time is over. Tell me of these images. These beaten kings, these broken emperors. Surely a man of your years will not be doing battle."

"All are mobilized now!"

"All but Watchers," I said. "Take a moment. Yearning for the past is born in me. Gormon has vanished; be my guide to these lost cycles."

The Rememberer shook his head wildly, circled around me, and tried to get away. Hoping to seize his skinny arm and pin him to the spot, I made a lunge at him; but he eluded me and I caught only his dark shawl, which pulled free and came loose in my hands. Then he was gone, his spindly limbs pumping madly as he fled down the street and left my view. I shrugged and examined the shawl I had so unexpectedly acquired. It was shot through with glimmering threads of metal arranged in intricate patterns that teased the eye: it seemed to me that each strand disappeared into the weave of the fabric, only to reappear at some improbable point, like the lineage of dynasties unexpectedly revived in distant cities. The workman-

ship was superb. Idly I draped the shawl about my shoulders.

I walked on.

My legs, which had been on the verge of failing me earlier in the day, now served me well. With renewed youthfulness I made my way through the chaotic city, finding no difficulties in choosing my route. I headed for the river, then crossed it and, on the Tver's far side, sought the palace of the Prince. The night had deepened, for most lights were extinguished under the mobilization orders; and from time to time a dull boom signaled the explosion of a screening bomb overhead, liberating clouds of murk that shielded the city from most forms of long-range scrutiny. There were fewer pedestrians in the streets. The sirens still cried out. Atop the buildings the defensive installations were going into action; I heard the bleeping sounds of repellors warming up, and I saw long spidery arms of amplification booms swinging from tower to tower as they linked for maximum output. I had no doubt now that the invasion actually was coming. My own instruments might have been fouled by inner confusion, but they would not have proceeded thus far with the mobilization if the initial report had not been confirmed by the findings of hundreds of other members of my guild.

As I neared the palace a pair of breathless Rememberers sped toward me, their shawls flapping behind them. They called to me in words I did not comprehend—some code of their guild, I realized, recollecting that I wore

Basil's shawl. I could not reply, and they rushed upon me, still gabbling; and switching to the language of ordinary men they said, "What is the matter with you? To your post! We must record! We must comment! We must observe!"

"You mistake me," I said mildly. "I keep this shawl only for your brother Basil, who left it in my care. I have no post to guard at this time."

"A Watcher," they cried in unison, and cursed me separately, and ran on. I laughed and went to the palace.

Its gates stood open. The neuters who had guarded the outer portal were gone, as were the two Indexers who had stood just within the door. The beggars that had thronged the vast plaza had jostled their way into the building itself to seek shelter; this had awakened the anger of the licensed hereditary mendicants whose customary stations were in that part of the building, and they had fallen upon the inflowing refugees with fury and unexpected strength. I saw cripples lashing out with their crutches held as clubs; I saw blind men landing blows with suspicious accuracy; meek penitents were wielding a variety of weapons ranging from stilettos to sonic pistols. Holding myself aloof from this shameless spectacle, I penetrated to the inner recesses of the palace and peered into chapels where I saw Pilgrims beseeching the blessings of the Will, and Communicants desperately seeking spiritual guidance as to the outcome of the coming conflict.

Abruptly I heard the blare of trumpets and cries of, "Make way! Make way!"

A file of sturdy Servitors marched into the palace, striding toward the Prince's chambers in the apse. Several of them held a struggling, kicking, frantic figure with half-unfolded wings: Avluela! I called out to her, but my voice died in the din, nor could I reach her. The Servitors shoved me aside. The procession vanished into the princely chambers. I caught a final glimpse of the little Flier, pale and small in the grip of her captors, and then she was gone once more.

I seized a bumbling neuter who had been moving uncertainly in the wake of the Servitors.

"That Flier! Why was she brought here?"

"He—he—they—"

"Tell me!"

"The Prince—his woman—in his chariot—he—he—they—the invaders—"

I pushed the flabby creature aside and rushed toward the apse. A brazen wall ten times my own height confronted me. I pounded on it. "Avluela!" I shouted hoarsely. *"Av . . . lu . . . ela . . . !"*

I was neither thrust away nor admitted. I was ignored. The bedlam at the western doors of the palace had extended itself now to the nave and aisles, and as the ragged beggars boiled toward me I executed a quick turn and found myself passing through one of the side doors of the palace.

Suspended and passive, I stood in the courtyard that led to the royal hostelry. A

strange electricity crackled in the air. I assumed it was an emanation from one of Roum's defense installations, some kind of beam designed to screen the city from attack. But an instant later I realized that it presaged the actual arrival of the invaders.

Starships blazed in the heavens.

When I had perceived them in my Watching they had appeared black against the infinite blackness, but now they burned with the radiance of suns. A stream of bright, hard, jewel-like globes bedecked the sky; they were ranged side by side, stretching from east to west in a continuous band, filling all the celestial arch, and as they erupted simultaneously into being it seemed to me that I heard the crash and throb of an invisible symphony heralding the arrival of the conquerors of Earth.

I do not know how far above me the starships were, nor how many of them hovered there, nor any of the details of their design. I know only that in sudden massive majesty they were there, and that if I had been a Defender my soul would have withered instantly at the sight.

Across the heavens shot light of many hues. The battle had been joined. I could not comprehend the actions of our warriors, and I was equally baffled by the maneuvers of those who had come to take possession of our history-crusted but time-diminished planet. To my shame I felt not only out of the struggle but above the struggle, as though this were no quarrel of mine. I wanted Avluela

beside me, and she was somewhere within the depths of the palace of the Prince of Roum. Even Gormon would have been a comfort now, Gormon the Changeling, Gormon the spy, Gormon the monstrous betrayer of our world.

Gigantic amplified voices bellowed, "Make way for the Prince of Roum! The Prince of Roum leads the Defenders in the battle for the fatherworld!"

From the palace emerged a shining vehicle the shape of a teardrop, in whose bright-metaled roof a transparent sheet had been mounted so that all the populace could see and take heart in the presence of the ruler. At the controls of the vehicle sat the Prince of Roum, proudly erect, his cruel, youthful features fixed in harsh determination; and beside him, robed like an empress, I beheld the slight figure of the Flier Avluela. She seemed in a trance.

The royal chariot soared upward and was lost in the darkness.

It seemed to me that a second vehicle appeared and followed its path, and that the Prince's reappeared, and that the two flew in tight circles, apparently locked in combat. Clouds of blue sparks wrapped both chariots now; and then they swung high and far and were lost to me behind one of the hills of Roum.

Was the battle now raging all over the planet? Was Perris in jeopardy, and holy Jorslem, and even the sleepy isles of the Lost Continents? Did starships hover everywhere?

I did not know. I perceived events in only one small segment of the sky over Roum, and even there my awareness of what was taking place was dim, uncertain, and ill-informed. There were momentary flashes of light in which I saw battalions of Fliers streaming across the sky; and then darkness returned as though a velvet shroud had been hurled over the city. I saw the great machines of our defense firing in fitful bursts from the tops of our towers; and yet I saw the starships untouched, unharmed, unmoved above. The courtyard in which I stood was deserted, but in the distance I heard voices, full of fear and foreboding, shouting in tinny tones that might have been the screeching of birds. Occasionally there came a booming sound that rocked all the city. Once a platoon of Somnambulists was driven past where I was; in the plaza fronting the palace I observed what appeared to be an array of Clowns unfolding some sort of sparkling netting of a military look; by one flash of lightning I was able to see a trio of Rememberers making copious notes of all that elapsed as they soared aloft on the gravity plate. It seemed—I was not sure—that the vehicle of the Prince of Roum returned, speeding across the sky with its pursuer clinging close. "Avluela," I whispered, as the twin dots of lights left my sight. Were the starships disgorging troops? Did colossal pylons of force spiral down from those orbiting brightnesses to touch the surface of the Earth? Why had the Prince seized Avluela? Where was Gormon? What were our

Defenders doing? Why were the enemy ships not blasted from the sky?

Rooted to the ancient cobbles of the courtyard, I observed the cosmic battle in total lack of understanding throughout the long night.

Dawn came. Strands of pale light looped from tower to tower. I touched fingers to my eyes, realizing that I must have slept while standing. Perhaps I should apply for membership in the guild of Somnambulists, I told myself lightly. I put my hands to the Rememberer's shawl about my shoulders and wondered how I managed to acquire it, and the answer came.

I looked toward the sky.

The alien starships were gone. I saw only the ordinary morning sky, gray with pinkness breaking through. I felt the jolt of compulsion and looked about for my cart, and reminded myself that I need do no more Watching, and I felt more empty than one would ordinarily feel at such an hour.

Was the battle over?

Had the enemy been vanquished?

Were the ships of the invaders blasted from the sky and lying in charred ruin outside Roum?

All was silent. I heard no more celestial symphonies. Then out of the eerie stillness there came a new sound, a rumbling noise as of wheeled vehicles passing through the streets of the city. And the invisible Musicians played one final note, deep and reso-

nant, which trailed away jaggedly as though every string had been broken at once.

Over the speakers used for public announcements came quiet words.

"Roum is fallen. Roum is fallen."

8

The royal hostelry was untended. Neuters and members of the servant guilds all had fled. Defenders, Masters, and Dominators must have perished honorably in combat. Basil the Rememberer was nowhere about; likewise none of his brethren. I went to my room, cleansed and refreshed and fed myself, gathered my few possessions, and bade farewell to the luxuries I had known so briefly. I regretted that I had had such a short time to visit Roum; but at least Gormon had been a most excellent guide, and I had seen a great deal.

Now I proposed to move on.

It did not seem prudent to remain in a conquered city. My room's thinking cap did not respond to my queries, and so I did not know what the extent of the defeat was, here or in other regions, but it was evident to me that Roum at least had passed from human con-

trol, and I wished to depart quickly. I weighed the thought of going to Jorslem, as that tall pilgrim had suggested upon my entry into Roum; but then I reflected and chose a westward route, toward Perris, which not only was closer but held the headquarters of the Rememberers. My own occupation had been destroyed; but on this first morning of Earth's conquest I felt a sudden powerful and strange yearning to offer myself humbly to the Rememberers and seek with them knowledge of our more glittering yesterdays.

At midday I left the hostelry. I walked first to the palace, which still stood open. The beggars lay strewn about, some drugged, some sleeping, most dead; from the crude manner of their death I saw that they must have slain one another in their panic and frenzy. A despondent-looking Indexer squatted beside the three skulls of the interrogation fixture in the chapel. As I entered he said, "No use. The brains do not reply."

"How goes it with the Prince of Roum?"

"Dead. The invaders shot him from the sky."

"A young Flier rode beside him. What do you know of her?"

"Nothing. Dead, I suppose."

"And the city?"

"Fallen. Invaders are everywhere."

"Killing?"

"Not even looting," the Indexer said. "They are most gentle. They have *collected* us."

"In Roum alone, or everywhere?"

The man shrugged. He began to rock rhyth-

mically back and forth. I let him be, and walked deeper into the palace. To my surprise, the imperial chambers of the Prince were unsealed. I went within; I was awed by the sumptuous luxury of the hangings, the draperies, the lights, the furnishings. I passed from room to room, coming at last to the royal bed, whose coverlet was the flesh of a colossal bivalve of the planet of another star, and as the shell yawned for me I touched the infinitely soft fabric under which the Prince of Roum had lain, and I recalled that Avluela too had lain here, and if I had been a younger man I would have wept.

I left the palace and slowly crossed the plaza to begin my journey toward Perris.

As I departed I had my first glimpse of our conquerors. A vehicle of alien design drew up at the plaza's rim and perhaps a dozen figures emerged. They might almost have been human. They were tall and broad, deep-chested, as Gormon had been, and only the extreme length of their arms marked them instantly as alien. Their skins were of strange texture, and if I had been closer I suspect I would have seen eyes and lips and nostrils that were not of a human design. Taking no notice of me, they crossed the plaza, walking in a curiously loose-jointed loping way that reminded me irresistibly of Gormon's stride, and entered the palace. They seemed neither swaggering nor belligerent.

Sightseers. Majestic Roum once more exerted its magnetism upon strangers.

Leaving our new masters to their amuse-

ment, I walked off, toward the outskirts of the city. The bleakness of eternal winter crept into my soul. I wondered: did I feel sorrow that Roum had fallen? Or did I mourn the loss of Avluela? Or was it only that I now had missed three successive Watchings, and like an addict I was experiencing the pangs of withdrawal?

It was all of these that pained me, I decided. But mostly the last.

No one was abroad in the city as I made for the gates. Fear of the new masters kept the Roumish in hiding, I supposed. From time to time one of the alien vehicles hummed past, but I was unmolested. I came to the city's western gate late in the afternoon. It was open, revealing to me a gently rising hill on whose breast rose trees with dark green crowns. I passed through and saw, a short distance beyond the gate, the figure of a Pilgrim who was shuffling slowly away from the city.

I overtook him easily.

His faltering, uncertain walk seemed strange to me, for not even his thick brown robes could hide the strength and youth of his body; he stood erect, his shoulders square and his back straight, and yet he walked with the hesitating, trembling step of an old man. When I drew abreast of him and peered under his hood I understood, for affixed to the bronze mask all Pilgrims wear was a reverberator, such as is used by blind men to warn them of obstacles and hazards. He became

aware of me and said, "I am a sightless Pilgrim. I pray you do not molest me."

It was not a Pilgrim's voice. It was a strong and harsh and imperious voice.

I replied, "I molest no one. I am a Watcher who has lost his occupation this night past."

"Many occupations were lost this night past, Watcher."

"Surely not a Pilgrim's."

"No," he said. "Not a Pilgrim's."

"Where are you bound?"

"Away from Roum."

"No particular destination?"

"No," the Pilgrim said. "None. I will wander."

"Perhaps we should wander together," I said, for it is accounted good luck to travel with a Pilgrim, and, shorn of my Flier and my Changeling, I would otherwise have traveled alone. "My destination is Perris. Will you come?"

"There as well as anywhere else," he said bitterly. "Yes. We will go to Perris together. But what business does a Watcher have there?"

"A Watcher has no business anywhere. I go to Perris to offer myself in service to the Rememberers."

"Ah," he said. "I was of that guild too, but it was only honorary."

"With Earth fallen, I wish to learn more of Earth in its pride."

"Is all Earth fallen, then, and not only Roum?"

"I think it is so," I said.

"Ah," replied the Pilgrim. "Ah!"

He fell silent and we went onward. I gave him my arm, and now he shuffled no longer, but moved with a young man's brisk stride. From time to time he uttered what might have been a sigh or a smothered sob. When I asked him details of his Pilgrimage, he answered obliquely or not at all. When we were an hour's journey outside Roum, and already amid forests, he said suddenly, "This mask gives me pain. Will you help me adjust it?"

To my amazement he began to remove it. I gasped, for it is forbidden for a Pilgrim to reveal his face. Had he forgotten that I was not sightless too?

As the mask came away he said, "You will not welcome this sight."

The bronze grillwork slipped down from his forehead, and I saw first eyes that had been newly blinded, gaping holes where no surgeon's knife, but possibly thrusting fingers, had penetrated, and then the sharp regal nose, and finally the quirked, taut lips of the Prince of Roum.

"Your Majesty!" I cried.

Trails of dried blood ran down his cheeks. About the raw sockets themselves were smears of ointment. He felt little pain, I suppose, for he had killed it with those green smears, but the pain that burst through me was real and potent.

"Majesty no longer," he said. "Help me with the mask!" His hands trembled as he held it forth. "These flanges must be widened. They press cruelly at my cheeks. Here—here—"

Quickly I made the adjustments, so that I would not have to see his ruined face for long.

He replaced the mask. "I am a Pilgrim now," he said quietly. "Roum is without its Prince. Betray me if you wish, Watcher; otherwise help me to Perris; and if ever I regain my power you will be well rewarded."

"I am no betrayer," I told him.

In silence we continued. I had no way of making small talk with such a man. It would be a somber journey for us to Perris; but I was committed now to be his guide. I thought of Gormon and how well he had kept his vows. I thought too of Avluela, and a hundred times the words leaped to my tongue to ask the fallen Prince how his consort the Flier had fared in the night of defeat, and I did not ask.

Twilight gathered, but the sun still gleamed golden-red before us in the west. And suddenly I halted and made a hoarse sound of surprise deep in my throat, as a shadow passed overhead.

High above me Avluela soared. Her skin was stained by the colors of the sunset, and her wings were spread to their fullest, radiant with every hue of the spectrum. She was already at least the height of a hundred men above the ground, and still climbing, and to her I must have been only a speck among the trees.

"What is it?" the Prince asked. "What do you see?"

"Nothing."

"Tell me what you see!"

I could not deceive him. "I see a Flier, your Majesty. A slim girl far aloft."

"Then the night must have come."

"No," I said. "The sun is still above the horizon."

"How can that be? She can have only nightwings. The sun would hurl her to the ground."

I hesitated. I could not bring myself to explain how it was that Avluela flew by day, though she had only nightwings. I could not tell the Prince of Roum that beside her, wingless, flew the invader Gormon, effortlessly moving through the air, his arm about her thin shoulders, steadying her, supporting her, helping her resist the pressure of the solar wind. I could not tell him that his nemesis flew with the last of his consorts above his head.

"Well?" he demanded. "How does she fly by day?"

"I do not know," I said. "It is a mystery to me. There are many things nowadays I can no longer understand."

The Prince appeared to accept that. "Yes, Watcher. Many things none of us can understand."

He fell once more into silence. I yearned to call out to Avluela, but I knew she could not and would not hear me, and so I walked on toward the sunset, toward Perris, leading the blind Prince. And over us Avluela and Gormon sped onward, limned sharply against the day's last glow, until they climbed so high they were lost to my sight.